The Pursuit

Nancy Rue

BETHANY HOUSE PUBLISHERS
MINNEAPOLIS, MINNESOTA 55438

The Pursuit

Nancy Rue

Published by Bethany House Publishers
A Ministry of Bethany Fellowship International
11400 Hampshire Avenue South
Minneapolis, Minnesota 55438
www.bethanyhouse.com

Printed in the United States of America by
Bethany Press International, Minneapolis, Minnesota 55438

Library of Congress Cataloging-in-Publication Data

Rue, Nancy N.
    The pursuit / Nancy Rue
        p. cm. — (Christian heritage series. The Chicago years ; bk. 6)
    Summary: While his family faces a series of problems in their Chicago home in 1929 and
as he enters junior high, Rudy struggles with the conflict between growing up and remaining
a kid.
    ISBN 1-56179-856-8
    [1. Family life—Fiction. 2. Christian life—Fiction. 3. Chicago (Ill.)—Fiction.] I. Title.
PZ7.R88515 Pu 2000
[Fic]—dc21   99-055398
                                                                                  CIP

---

00   01   02   03   04   /   10   9   8   7   6   5   4   3   2   1

*For Kelly Gordon, who is always
in pursuit of the best she can be.*

Chapter One

*I*t was dark in the Berghoff German Restaurant that afternoon with the stained-glass windows and the polished wood paneling. At least it was dark enough for Rudy Hutchinson to think he could slip some salt into the sugar bowl before his great-aunt Gussie sweetened her coffee.

As usual, he was wrong. Not only was the iron-haired Aunt Gussie just as sharp in the dimly-lit restaurant as she was in broad daylight; this time she had help. Just as she was about to dump a spoonful of salty sugar into her cup, she brought it up close to her wire-rimmed glasses and inspected it.

"What's the matter, Aunt Gussie?" Rudy said innocently. "Is there a bug in it or something?"

"A bug, my foot," said an unfamiliar voice at his elbow.

Rudy looked up to see a blonde girl paused by their table with an empty tray resting on her hip. The sprinkle of freckles on her nose gave away her youthfulness, but the hard, no-nonsense look in her eyes put her right up there in Aunt Gussie's 60s.

"I beg your pardon?" Aunt Gussie said.

"There's no bug in your sugar, madam," the girl said. "We don't

1

allow bugs here at the Berghoff. But there is some salt that *he* poured in there when you were looking at the dessert menu."

"Is that so?" Aunt Gussie said.

Her voice hadn't come to a point yet, and neither had her eyes. There was still a good chance she'd fall for it. Rudy leaned slightly over the table and said, "Come on, Aunt Gussie. You know I don't do that kind of thing anymore."

"Suit yourself," the girl said, and she started to move on.

But Aunt Gussie put up a finger, and the girl waited. In fact, it seemed as though the entire restaurant waited, because when Gustavia Nitz gave a command, everybody within looking distance obeyed.

Uh-oh, Rudy thought. *Maybe this wasn't such a hot idea after all.*

And this time he was right. Aunt Gussie touched the tip of her finger into the spoon with the class of a queen, licked it delicately, and set the spoon down on her saucer.

"It was just a joke," Rudy said. "I knew you wouldn't actually put it in your cup. And if you had, I'd have stopped you before you drank it."

"Applesauce," said the blonde girl. "But then, that's just my opinion. Now if you'll hand me that sugar bowl, sonny, I'll get your aunt another one."

"Just a moment, my dear," Aunt Gussie said. "What is your name, if you don't mind my asking?"

What's this about? Rudy thought. Of course, it was about *something*. Aunt Gussie always said there were two things she never wasted: her time and her breath.

"I don't mind at all," the girl said. "I'm Ingrid Feilchenfeld."

"Good German name," Aunt Gussie said. Her sharp eyes were shining with approval.

"My father was one of the few Germans who refused to change his name during the war when everyone wanted us all shipped out of America."

"That was utter nonsense, that business about German-Americans being a threat to the native-born," Aunt Gussie said. "That makes as much sense as saying we should deport all our Italian-Americans because Al Capone is Italian."

"That's right!" Rudy said—as much to get back into Aunt Gussie's good graces as to defend his adopted brother, Little Al Delgado.

Either way, Aunt Gussie didn't seem impressed, at least not with Rudy. She did have a smile for Ingrid, though.

"You're a very mature young woman for your age," she said.

Ingrid just nodded her thanks.

She sure thinks highly of herself, Rudy thought. He busied himself with the remains of his chicken schnitzel so Ingrid wouldn't see his cheeks turning red. He was suddenly feeling like a chump in front of her.

"How do you account," Aunt Gussie said, "for the fact that you can't be a day over 17 and yet you act as if you're 30? There is none of that shrieking and squealing most girls your age do these days."

She sits around reading Emily Post, Rudy thought.

"My father is an old-stock German," Ingrid said, eyes lighting up proudly. Rudy noticed that they couldn't decide whether to be blue or green. "He raised me to be law-abiding, church-going—"

"And obviously hard-working," Aunt Gussie put in.

"Then during the War, when everyone turned on us for being German, he said I had to be more than just that. I had to grow up fast and be strong enough to stand up for who I am."

"I certainly wish more people would bring their children up that way," Aunt Gussie said.

I was brought up that way! Rudy wanted to say. But that wouldn't exactly have been true. Until a little over a year ago, Rudy and his twin sister, Hildy Helen, had been raised by their lawyer father, since their mother had died when they were small. Dad loved them, of course, but he had always been so busy with his cases back in Shelbyville, Indiana, Hildy Helen and Rudy had been left to their own mischief much of the time.

That was until Dad brought them to Chicago to live with Aunt Gussie. Dad still worked hard in the city as a pro-bono lawyer, taking cases for people who couldn't afford to pay him. But Aunt Gussie hadn't left the twins on their own, not for a minute. Law-abiding, church-going—Rudy and Hildy Helen had become both of those things. They had no choice.

"So what does that mean, standing up for who you are?" Aunt Gussie said.

Ingrid laughed from deep down in her throat. "I refuse to call a frankfurter a hot dog or a hamburger a Salisbury steak!" she said. "I won't apologize for being German."

"But I *will* apologize for your waitress standing at your table yapping!"

The white-haired German lady with the thick accent who had checked Aunt Gussie's walking stick and hat for her when they'd arrived was now swooping down on them with her eyes blazing at Ingrid.

"My fault entirely," Aunt Gussie said. "I was enjoying our discussion. It is so refreshing to have a conversation with a young woman that isn't punctuated with 'nifty' and 'the bee's knees' and half a dozen other expressions I can't make heads nor tails of."

The German woman gave a sympathetic growl and asked Aunt Gussie if she had enjoyed her sauerbraten. With a final look down her freckled nose at Rudy, Ingrid shifted her tray to her other curvy hip and hurried away, and Rudy watched her go. She was short, but Aunt Gussie was right—she did look like a grown-up—not like LaDonna Hutchinson, Rudy's 17-year-old cousin, who was tall and willowy and angel-faced.

"Some strudel for you now?" the German lady said.

Rudy was sure Aunt Gussie was going to say no and then drag him out of the Berghoff by the ear and chew him out for making an idiot out of himself in such a classy restaurant. But she nodded at the woman and said, "Make it two. And a coffee with lots of milk for my nephew."

When she was gone, Aunt Gussie gave Rudy a dry look. "I'd be careful before I put any sugar in it though," she said.

Rudy felt his face fill up with color again. "I'm sorry, Aunt Gussie," he said.

Aunt Gussie laced the fingers of her blue-veined hands and rested them on the table. "What was that all about, Rudolph?" she said. "I can't remember the last time you attempted to play a prank on me."

Rudy tried to shrug it off, but Aunt Gussie wasn't buying it.

"You say you don't know," she said, "but I think you do." She sighed. "Looks as if I'll have to pry it out of you."

"I really don't know!" Rudy said. "I just felt like doing something—I don't know—"

"Mischievous?" Aunt Gussie said.

"I guess."

"Even after we just spent two lovely hours in the Art Institute—at *your* request, I might remind you."

"I know. And it was swell! Did I tell you about that one Picasso I saw, the one with the lady with the cats? I wanted to tell you what I thought."

"In a moment, yes, after we sort this out," Aunt Gussie said.

Rudy looked down at his own hands, as always marked with an ink stain on his knuckle from drawing. Sitting at a table talking about Picasso and Charlie Chaplin and the White Sox while they ate schnitzel and she treated him like an adult—these were his favorite times with Aunt Gussie. He felt like a chump for spoiling it.

"And then I bought you new school clothes and all the supplies you're going to need for junior high," Aunt Gussie was saying. She stopped and surveyed him carefully from behind her spectacles. "Does this sudden immature behavior have anything to do with your starting school this week? Are you perhaps a little nervous about all that's going to be expected of you this year?"

Rudy wished that lady would get back with the strudel. He really didn't want to answer this question.

"Well?"

"Everybody is making it out to be so important," Rudy said finally. "All the changing classrooms and wearing different clothes for gym and trying to keep up with the homework and the eighth and ninth graders picking on you in the halls. I don't see what the big deal is."

"Then there must be some other explanation for why your mouth is so dry your lips are smacking when you talk. Take a sip of water, Rudolph, and listen to me."

Rudy, of course, did.

" 'Everybody'—by whom you mean your father and Miss Tibbs—is making junior high out to be important because it is. It's a big step in your education."

"I wish they had never built Hirsch Junior High. I wish we could go to Felthensal two more years like they used to."

"You'd have to start high school eventually," Aunt Gussie said. "And I understand the students who have had the junior high experience these past three years have adjusted much better to the rigors of high school when they got there."

"I'd rather wait," Rudy mumbled.

"Which is why you're going back to your old little-boy behaviors. The salt in the sugar bowl. The frog in the backseat of the Pierce Arrow."

"You saw that?" Rudy gulped. "Open your handbag really careful then," he said. "There's a cricket in there."

"After I found the frog, I checked my handbag straight away. But thank you for your honesty."

Rudy resisted the urge to plant his elbows on the table and sink his face in his hands. "So what's my punishment going to be?"

he said.

"None. I am only going to reassure you, Rudolph, that you are ready for junior high school, and you will most certainly rise to the occasion."

"I bet Little Al and Hildy Helen aren't nervous."

Aunt Gussie seemed to be withholding a smile. "Hildegarde is not, no. She is far too excited about the prospect of handsome young men gathering from all over the city to be the slightest bit afraid."

"What does she want handsome young men for?" Rudy said. "She's got me and Al."

"Al and me—and I don't think her two brothers, handsome though they may be, meet her requirements for romance."

"Romance? That's a bunch of hooey!"

"As for Alonzo, he wouldn't admit he was nervous if his life depended on it. When he and I went on our outing, he could talk of almost nothing but how impressed I am going to be at his academic performance."

"What's academic performance?"

"His grades."

"I wouldn't hold my breath, Aunt Gussie."

"I know," she said, "but I intend to give him all the help and support I can. His early education was so neglected. He has a great deal of catching up to do."

"I'll help him, too," Rudy said.

"After you tend to your own studies," Aunt Gussie said. Her face became stern. "You are bright, Rudolph. You have an intelligence that no one so far has challenged you to live up to, including Miss Tibbs. I know she and your father are keeping company now, so I don't want to say anything against her, but she didn't force you to work to your potential in the sixth grade. I have been praying that you will sit under at least one teacher this year who does."

Rudy didn't like the sound of that. As close as Aunt Gussie was to God, if she prayed for something, it was bound to come true. Just hearing all that stuff about potential and challenge made him more anxious than ever. His fingers inched toward the straw in his glass. He was itching to shoot it across the room and through the feathers on that club lady's hat.

"Don't even consider it, Rudolph," Aunt Gussie said dryly. "It is perfectly normal for you to be nervous, and I'm glad that you've shared that with me. I'm here to help you in any way I can, but that does not include bailing you out of situations you have gotten yourself into foolishly and unnecessarily. Are we clear?"

"Yes, Aunt Gussie," Rudy said.

And then, thank the Lord, the strudels arrived.

When they had both cleaned their bowls down to the design on the china, Aunt Gussie suggested a brisk walk to help them digest all that heavy German food. Rudy groaned silently. It was at least 90 degrees, and when it was that hot in Chicago, even in September, the street could feel like a griddle ready to grill your feet right through your shoes.

At least since her stroke last winter, Aunt Gussie couldn't trot quite as "briskly" as she had been able to before. Still, armed with her carved walking stick, she could make a person work up a sweat, and she did as she led Rudy down Adams Street to Michigan Avenue where they turned toward the Chicago River.

"It's always cooler on the water," Aunt Gussie said.

Rudy licked the beads of perspiration from his upper lip and hoped so. He tried to concentrate on the people passing so he wouldn't think so much about the way he was broiling inside his starched collar.

There were plenty of other men broiling as well in their starched collars and their vests and their hats. The women didn't look any more comfortable, sporting helmet-style hats that fit tightly on their heads and came down to the napes of their necks. At least their legs were bare, and Rudy noticed that a lot of them, on the younger women, were fashionably suntanned from their summer vacations.

Too bad the summer's over, Rudy thought. *I'd much rather be back at Cape Cod than starting junior high.*

But it was no good thinking about it, and he focused his attention on the new office building that was going up, rising like a cage of steel into the city sky to join the others.

"That infernal racket!" Aunt Gussie said as soon as she could be heard above the riveters.

"I heard on the radio that that's the sound of progress," Rudy said.

"Hmm," Aunt Gussie said. That was one thing about Aunt Gussie. You couldn't call her old-fashioned. She listened to every new idea, and if it made sense and didn't go against the Bible, she adopted it. But if it didn't, look out.

The thought had no sooner crossed Rudy's mind than Aunt Gussie was stopping him with a firm hand and pointing to an open doorway which was crowded with people.

"What's going on in there?" Rudy said.

"That is a stock broker's office, Rudolph," she said. She glanced up at the clock on the corner. "It is now the noon hour, and all these people are checking to see how their fortunes are faring."

Rudy stood on tiptoes and craned his neck to see what men with fortunes looked like. Every seat inside the office was taken, and there were men and women lining the walls as well as crowding into the doorway. They all seemed to be staring at something.

"What are they looking at?" Rudy said.

"You see that translux screen up there?"

Rudy nodded. There was something like a small moving picture screen with the date September 3, 1929, at the top of it and an endless procession of letters and figures running across it.

"That is a record of all the buying and selling that is going on at the New York Stock Exchange," Aunt Gussie said. "Minute by minute these people who have invested their money in the stock market can see whether the price of their stock is rising or falling. If it goes high, they can sell for much more than they purchased for and make a fortune. If it falls, they stand to lose a great deal of money."

"Nobody's losing any money today, lady," said a man standing nearby. Rudy was startled. The man was wearing what looked like a janitor's uniform. "Prices are the highest they've been yet. I just bought stock a month ago at eight dollars a share, and now it's $115 a share! I just made me a bundle!"

As he moved away, Aunt Gussie shook her head. "And I bet he either borrowed the money or used his entire life savings to do it. I read in the *Fortune* magazine that there are six billion dollars outstanding in brokers' loans."

"Now what's happening?" Rudy said, for a murmur went through the crowd and the screen seemed to be going crazy.

"Who can tell?" said a woman in a white starched uniform and white stockings. "The ticker's having a hard time keeping up with the trading, it's going so fast."

The man beside her grinned broadly in spite of the sweat that soaked the front of his gasoline attendant's shirt. "Ain't it great!" he said. "Everybody oughta be rich!"

Aunt Gussie nudged Rudy out of the crowd and didn't speak again until they were almost to the bridge. Rudy could tell by the way she was thumping her walking stick that the scene at the broker's office had her worked up.

"Horse feathers on the Get-Rich-Quick Era!" she said finally. "The trouble is, everybody *isn't* rich. But those foolhardy people who have thrown all their money—and all their credit—into the stock market aren't thinking about the wheat and corn farmers in the Midwest or the textile workers in New England or the sharecroppers in the Deep South. What about the men in the mines and the mills who are hardly earning enough to feed their families? Or our Negroes? Or our recent immigrants? None of them are getting rich. They're starving!"

Rudy wasn't sure what he was supposed to say, so he just nodded.

"I know you don't understand all of this, Rudolph," she said. "But you just mark my words: This is all going to come tumbling down sooner or later. What if all those shareholders decide to sell at once? You can't have a nation base its principles on money and what it can buy and not be sorry in the long run."

She shook her head again, and she was about to thump on with Rudy trotting dutifully beside her when there was a squeal of tires behind them. Rudy whirled around in time to see a black Dodge fishtail around the corner with a new Plymouth right on its bumper.

From somewhere in the distance a siren was wailing, but the occupants of the two cars obviously weren't worried about that. The passenger door of the Plymouth flew open and a man in tinted glasses leapt out onto the running board and hung on while he groped inside his jacket.

"He's going for his gun!" someone screamed on the street.

There was a frantic rush for doorways. Rudy grabbed Aunt Gussie's arm just as a shot rang out from the window of the Dodge.

"Get inside!" he cried.

But Aunt Gussie was having a hard time getting herself turned around, and the walking stick got tangled between her legs. She swayed and started to fall.

"Here!" a man's voice shouted. "I've got her!"

Rudy pushed her in the direction of the voice just as he felt the Dodge narrowly miss him. He tried to push himself through the crowd to follow Aunt Gussie, but another shot rang out, and a sharp pop ripped the air.

Rudy whipped his head around. The Plymouth was out of control and was swerving crazily up onto the sidewalk. He made one more mad lunge for Aunt Gussie, but it was too late. Hard metal hit him in the backside, and Rudy went sailing into the crowd.

Chapter Two

*R*udy never hit the ground. His fall was broken by the mass of bodies still trying to cram its way into a sandwich shop.

"Whoa there, young fella!" an elderly gentleman said as he helped Rudy pull himself up. "Are you all right there?"

Rudy had no idea. He was too stunned to know if anything hurt or even if he was still in one complete piece. He rubbed his backside vaguely and stretched his neck to look for Aunt Gussie.

There she was, lying stiff and gray-faced on the sidewalk.

After that, Rudy never thought about whether he was all right or not.

She wasn't dead. The ambulance attendant assured him of that.

And she hadn't even been hit by the Plymouth, which had finally lodged itself in the front window of a shoe store and dumped its occupants out into the waiting arms of a swarm of policemen.

"She's suffered a stroke," said the doctor in the ambulance.

"And it's no wonder!" That came from a man whose voice Rudy might have remembered if he hadn't been bewildered by the sirens and the shouting and especially the silence coming from Aunt Gussie. He was the man who had caught her when she'd started to fall.

"She never hit the sidewalk," the man said. "She was standing on her own two feet when she saw the boy here fly through the air. Then she stiffened up like a corpse and went down—*boom*—just like that."

"But she isn't a corpse, Rudy," said yet another voice. "She's had a stroke before, and she pulled out of it just fine. She'll be all right."

This was a voice Rudy did recognize, and he sank against its owner like a balloon losing air. It was Detective Zorn, a friend of his dad's—a friend of all the Hutchinsons, and a kinder and wiser man they'd never had in their home. If Detective Zorn said it was going to be all right, then it was.

But Rudy soon realized that this time Detective Zorn had it wrong.

Rudy knew that the minute his father came to him in the hospital, where a doctor wearing a pince nez had just examined his backside and pronounced it merely bruised. Dad nodded gratefully at that news and said, "Let's go home, Rudy."

The entire time Sol, Aunt Gussie's chauffeur, was driving them back to Prairie Avenue, Dad was silent, his mouth stiff, his eyes somber behind his wire-rimmed glasses. Rudy's own glasses were bent from his crash, and his knickers were torn, and his curly brown hair was hanging down in his eyes. But he couldn't think about any of that. He could only think: *She's dead. She must be dead. Please, God, don't let her be dead.*

"Daddy!" Hildy Helen cried when they walked in the front door. "Is Aunt Gussie dead? Please tell me she didn't die!"

Dad pulled Hildy Helen against the front of his now-wilted shirt and stroked her dark, shiny bob of hair. "She's not dead," he said. "But it's very serious."

"How serious, Mister James?" Quintonia said. The black maid's face was starched with concern. "Don't you hold anything back. How serious is it?"

LaDonna, Quintonia's niece, put her hand on her aunt's arm, but Quintonia wrenched it away and stood there in front of Dad as if he were about to rob her blind and she wasn't having it. All the Hutchinsons loved Aunt Gussie, but probably none of them more than Quintonia, who had been with her all her life.

"You know something?" said Miss Tibbs. "I think we all ought to gather in the sitting room and hear what Jim has to say."

Miss Tibbs had been Little Al and Hildy Helen and Rudy's teacher the year before. But now she was Dad's "companion," as he always called her. Just as Aunt Gussie would have done, Miss Tibbs ushered them all into the sitting room with its Oriental rug and its teakwood piano and all the other treasures Aunt Gussie had collected from her travels around the world.

It was suddenly strange. Rudy had been living in this house for over a year and had walked past the 18th-century fireplace andirons and the Grecian water jar and the wooden sculpture from the Congo hundreds of times. But right now, they all seemed to be straining toward him, crying, "Rudy! Where's Aunt Gussie? Isn't she coming home?"

"Isn't she coming home?" Rudy suddenly burst out.

"I wish you'd sit down first, Rudy," Miss Tibbs said, tilting her sandy-blonde head of closely cropped hair to the side.

And I wish you'd quit bossing me around! Rudy wanted to shout at her. *I just want to know what's happened to Aunt Gussie!*

Miss Tibbs's green eyes with their flecks of gold looked stung, as if she could read Rudy's face. She sat down on the chair by the fireplace, next to where Dad was standing, and looked down at her hands in her lap.

Hildy Helen crowded between Little Al and Rudy on the black horsehair sofa and wrung her own hands as if they were dishrags in Quintonia's kitchen. "Daddy, please—" she said.

"Aunt Gussie has had another stroke," he said.

"Miss Gustavio's a tough old doll!" Little Al said. He tossed his black hair and nudged Rudy with his sturdy elbow. "She'll get through it just like last time, Rudolpho. You can mark it."

His voice had its usual bright charm, but the eyes that begged for Rudy to agree with him were dark with fear. Aunt Gussie had been right—Little Al wouldn't admit he was afraid if his life depended on it. But his eyes were giving him away.

"Mark it," Little Al said. "I know that's gangster talk, but it fits here, is what I say. It means, it will happen. You can count on it."

"This stroke is much more serious than the last one," Dad said. "She's completely paralyzed on her left side and—" Dad stopped as if he'd run out of breath. "And she's unable to speak."

It was suddenly as if everyone in the room were rendered speechless, too. The thought of Aunt Gussie's not being able to breeze into a room with her opinions flying about her like colorful scarves left them all with nothing to say.

"Forever?" Hildy Helen said finally.

"The doctors don't know," Dad said. "There's a chance, of course, but most people never recover from a stroke of this severity—"

"But Miss Gustavio, she ain't most people!" Little Al said. He was starting to sound angry now.

"That's certainly true, Al," Miss Tibbs said. "If anyone can come back strong, it's Miss Gussie. We have to hang onto that with all our prayers."

Dad cleared his throat. "But in the meantime, I'm going to need your help."

"Whatever you want!" Hildy Helen said. She shoved her bobbed hair behind her ears the way a boy about to fight a bully would roll up his sleeves. "I can go to the hospital every day and read to her and talk to her. I'll even quit school if I have to—"

Dad's face twitched out of its pinched-tight mask of worry, and he almost smiled. "That won't be necessary, Hildy, but thank you. Now just hear me out, all of you."

Hildy Helen settled back beside Rudy and wrapped her fingers around his wrist. He could feel her pulse racing—or was it his?

"The federal government has set up a special task force to find a way to put Al Capone away for good. Not just this little jail term he's serving in Philadelphia now but a federal prison for the rest of his life."

"Excuse me, Mr. James, but what's that got to do with Miss Gussie?" Quintonia said. She was looking a little disgusted.

"Because I have agreed to assist the head of the task force, Mr. Ness," Dad said. "As you know, I—well, all of us as a family—have had our run-ins with Capone and his Mob. Today, although it was accidental that we were involved, was just one more example. Mr. Ness feels that I can help put Capone away for good by making a statement about what I know."

"But I still don't see—"

LaDonna turned to Quintonia. "It means Mr. Jim is going to be working harder than ever trying to put this all together. I'm going to continue helping him, of course."

"*While* you are finishing your last year of high school," Dad said. His voice was firm. "And there will be no argument, LaDonna. You have an excellent mind, and if you want to be a lawyer yourself as you say you do, you're going to have to finish school."

"Fine," LaDonna said. She picked a piece of lint from her beige linen suit. "But I will not become some prom trotter. I'm going to go to classes, and I'm going to work for you. That's all. That's the way Miss Gussie would want it."

Dad nodded, and then he looked at the children on the sofa. "But that means LaDonna won't have time to help much around here, and neither will Quintonia. Dr. Kennedy has assured me that as soon as Aunt Gussie is completely stable, he will allow her to come home. Quintonia, I think, is the best person to take care of her until Bridget finishes nursing school and perhaps comes back."

"Quintonia certainly is the best person to take care of her," Quintonia herself said. "And nobody else better even argue with that."

Nobody dared. Rudy found himself nodding enthusiastically.

"I'll be around to help when I'm not at school," Miss Tibbs said. "I know I'm not Aunt Gussie, and I won't even try to take her place, but—"

"You won't have to take her place, Miss Tibbsy," Little Al said fiercely, "'cause she ain't goin' nowhere!"

"Right," Miss Tibbs said, and she went back to looking at her hands.

"I gave this serious thought on the way home from the hospital," Dad said, "and I have come up with a single responsibility for each of you children. With school starting, this will be more than enough for you to handle."

The trio straightened on the sofa. Little Al was already clenching his fists for the job ahead.

"You can count on us to keep things percolatin' around here, Mr. Hutchie," he said.

"Hildy Helen," said Dad, "you will help out in the kitchen as much as possible. Quintonia will still cook, and Miss Tibbs will be here every evening to help, but they'll need your assistance. You'll work as a team."

Hildy Helen nodded, biting her lip.

"Little Al, can I count on you to look after Picasso?"

"And how, Mr. Hutchie!" Little Al said. "Me and that parrot'll be like this." He crossed his fingers. "And he won't miss Miss Gustavio one bit."

Rudy doubted that. Aunt Gussie's parrot *lived* to see her walk into the library and talk to him about ballet and opera and F. Scott Fitzgerald. Rudy's chest suddenly hurt. Aunt Gussie wasn't going to talk to Picasso about anything—maybe not ever.

"I want you to work with Sol, Rudy," Dad said. "We all have very busy schedules, and Aunt Gussie has always kept up with getting everyone everywhere he or she needs to be at the right time. Sol is getting old and deaf. He can't handle all that on his own. I want you to make sure he knows who to pick up where and when. Can you do that?"

Rudy nodded, but his head was heavy. He wasn't quite sure what he was agreeing to.

When the family meeting was over, Rudy wandered into the library and switched on the radio. It was time for the news. Aunt Gussie never missed Walter Winchell.

The familiar rapid-fire voice was just announcing that over eight million shares had been traded on the New York Stock Exchange that day, when Dad came in and turned the radio off. The horn-like speakers went silent.

"Aunt Gussie always listens to the news about now," Rudy said. "She'll want to know what's been going on when she comes home."

"Maybe she will," Dad said.

His face was pale, and a lock of dark, wavy hair was falling over onto his forehead just the way Rudy's hair did. He had long since taken off his jacket and vest. His striped shirt was rumpled, and one suspender was sagging from his shoulder. He didn't look young to Rudy just then. He looked old and tired.

"But there's a chance that she won't, Rudy," Dad said. "I want you to pray and have faith. But I also want you to be able to accept it if she can't respond to us. I know that's going to be especially hard for you, and that's why I want to talk to you."

"Talk, Dad," said Picasso from his cage. "Talk!"

"Yeah, talk, Dad," Rudy said, and he tried to smile. But his face just wouldn't move that way.

"You remember this summer," Dad said, "you tried to take on far too much responsibility."

"Yeah."

"I don't want you to try to do that, not even under these circumstances."

Rudy nodded, but once again, he wasn't quite sure what he was agreeing to. *Aunt Gussie told me to act mature and not like a little kid. Dad's telling me not to try to act like an adult. I don't think I get this.*

"And there's another thing," Dad said. "I don't want you getting any mistaken idea that your aunt's illness is your fault. You were both innocent bystanders in an incident that should never have happened in the first place. We don't know for certain if the stroke occurred because she was so frightened by your being hit by the car. It might also have happened if you'd been riding peacefully along with her and Sol in the Pierce Arrow." Dad's thin lips came together in a line for a moment. "We may never know for sure, son," he said. "She may never be able to tell us. But either way, it was *not* your fault. Do you understand?"

Rudy nodded. This time he did agree, but the large lump in his throat kept him from answering. Dad squeezed his shoulder.

"You've come so far, Rudy," he said. "I'm awfully proud of you. Awfully proud."

He left the room then and quietly snapped the library door closed behind him.

He thinks I'm gonna cry in here, but I'm not, Rudy thought.

And he probably wouldn't have. He might actually have swallowed down that lump and turned the radio back on and listened to Walter Winchell spit out the news.

But Picasso chose just then to cock his head at Rudy and say, "Gustavia? Where is Gustavia Nitz?"

Rudy couldn't hold the tears back any longer.

And he didn't do much better the next day when Dad took the children to St. Luke's Hospital and one by one let them go into Aunt Gussie's room to say hello. Rudy went first, because he thought he should. Aunt Gussie would expect that.

As he pushed open the door with its foggy upper glass, Rudy tried to shake off his confusion about how he was supposed to behave. He shut the door carefully behind him, which gave him a little more time before he had to look at his aunt.

When he finally moved to her bed and saw her face, he wished he'd waited longer—maybe even forever.

The left side of her face was droopy and slack, so that her mouth—that firm, stern mouth that had been pulling him into shape for the last year of his life—was letting drool run off onto the pillow. Her sharp left eye sagged at the corner, and if she recognized him through it, she didn't show it. In fact, she closed it and let out a long, shuddering sigh that went through Rudy like a dull knife.

This was not the woman who practically ran Women for World Peace and the Chicago Women's Network and worked every day at Hull House, a training center for immigrants.

But Rudy took a deep breath and said, "Hello, Aunt Gussie," anyway.

Nothing.

"I just came to tell you—um—"

Tell me what, Rudolph? Come on, boy, out with it. There's no need for all this shilly-shallying around.

That was what he wished she'd say. He wished she would lift that limp left arm and wag her finger at him. He would have stood there all day and let her scold him, if only she would.

But her eyes stayed closed, and her mouth soaked the pillow-case, and the only sound she made was another long sigh.

"Open your eyes, Aunt Gussie!" Rudy said. "And I'll tell you what happened on the stock market yesterday!"

She didn't move.

"All right, I'll tell you anyway. They traded around more than eight million shares! I don't know what that means, but I bet it isn't good, and I thought you should know."

He watched her face. The right side twitched, but that was all.

I guess she's asleep, Rudy thought. *Nobody talks when they're asleep, right?*

But just as he turned to go, he saw a tear trickle out of Aunt Gussie's right eye and travel sadly down the side of her face.

Then he couldn't hold back the sobs any longer. He put his head down on her bed and cried for a long time. He cried because Aunt Gussie was sick. He cried because he didn't know what he'd do without her. He cried because the responsibility of making sure everyone else was okay was just too much. When he was through crying, he only knew one thing.

He couldn't be the mature young man Aunt Gussie wanted him to be. He just couldn't.

Chapter Three

*T*he children didn't go back to see Aunt Gussie after that. Dad took one look at their tear-stained faces and said they would wait until she came home.

Rudy didn't know whether to be relieved or angry over that decision. He didn't understand much about any of his feelings lately, and that made the first day of junior high even more threatening.

What if I just bust out crying in one of my classes? he asked himself as he stood in front of the bathroom mirror that morning and tried to slick his unruly, curly hair down the way Little Al did his straight, thick mop. *What if I don't understand a single thing the teachers say? Am I supposed to be mature and pretend I do, or do I stick my hand up like some kindergarten kid and look dumb in front of the class?*

He gave up on slicking down his hair, and he decided to give up on trying to be mature, too. He already knew that was a lost cause.

Miss Tibbs came by before she reported to her own school that morning and saw them off at the front door when they left to catch the bus. It had always been Aunt Gussie's job to check their faces and their hair and their teeth before they headed for school, and Rudy stiffened when Miss Tibbs said, "You look mighty handsome, Rudy."

"Yeah, I guess," he mumbled.

"What about me, Miss Tibbsy?" Little Al said.

"You look divine."

"I'd look a lot better in a pair a oxford bags—gray flannel. But Miss Gustavio said nothin' but knickers 'til I'm 14. Fourteen!"

"Then knickers it is," Miss Tibbs said. "She's still the boss around here."

Yes, she is, Rudy thought. *And don't you forget it!*

They had to go two blocks down the street, still wet from the nighttime street cleaner, to get to the bus stop, and Rudy looked wistfully back over his shoulder at the way they used to walk to get to Felthensal Grammar School. Life had sure been a lot easier back then.

"Everybody got their money for the bus?" Hildy Helen said.

"Got my money. Got my lunch," Little Al said.

Hildy Helen frowned. "Can you believe we have to carry our lunches?"

"Yeah, I'd rather come home for lunch like we did last year," Rudy said.

"I'd rather buy ours in the cafeteria. I bet that little snob Dorothea Worthington buys her lunch."

Little Al gave a satisfied smile. "Yeah, but at least we don't gotta put up with her brother this year. I'll always be grateful to Miss Tibbsy for not promotin' him to seventh grade. I like a doll like her."

Rudy had to admit that was one bright spot in what lay ahead. The Hutchinsons had suffered so much bullying from Maury Worthington, it might be worth going to a new school just to get away from him.

As they jammed into one seat on the crowded bus, Hildy Helen pulled in her chin so she could look at Rudy.

"You sure aren't excited about this, are you?" she said.

"No."

"You think it's going to be hard? LaDonna says seventh grade isn't that much harder than sixth."

"I don't care how hard it is," Little Al said. "I'm gonna study my backside off and get me a good education so I can get a decent job like Mr. Hutchie's got. I figure it's worth it if I don't gotta go sell two-cent papers or shine shoes like the kids from my old neighborhood—at least, the ones that don't go into crime, if you know what I mean."

Rudy definitely knew what he meant. Aunt Gussie had rescued Little Al from becoming just like Al Capone, and it was only because of her and Dad that he wasn't in Joliet Prison instead of Hirsch Junior High School. If he got into even a little bit of trouble, the judge would pluck him right out of his desk and drop him into a cell.

"Oh, brother," Hildy Helen said just then.

Rudy looked up to see her standing, face pressed against the window. They were just arriving at the school.

"What's the matter?" Rudy said.

And then he saw for himself. Standing smack in the middle of the front steps—where everyone could get a good view of her—was Dorothea Worthington.

"Isn't there a side entrance we can go into?" Hildy Helen said.

But there was no such luck. There was nothing they could do but try to walk right past her, and of course she didn't let that happen.

"Hello, *Hutchinsons*," she said, as if their last name were some nasty word.

Hildy Helen rolled her eyes at the boys and stopped. "Hello," she said.

Dorothea squinted her pale eyes at the boys. Dorothea always squinted, because she refused to wear the glasses she needed. Rudy straightened his own glasses and squinted back at her.

"I suppose you're staring at my new clothes," she said, tossing her almost colorless shock of boyish hair.

Rudy hadn't been, but he looked at them now. She was wearing a frock of different shades of green and brown jersey, like the stuff his bathing suit was made out of, and a gold belt that fastened around her hips and a long string of beads, which she was toying with as if she had practiced doing it in front of a mirror. But what really made Rudy groan inside were the shoes. He looked over at Hildy Helen.

Sure enough, she was looking at them, too, with her brown eyes in slits and nearly turning green with envy. They were the latest thing—pointy-toed, strapped Mary Janes with little bows on them, something Aunt Gussie would never have let Hildy wear to school, much less with flesh-colored rayon stockings, if they were the last pair of shoes in the store. *Utterly ridiculous for the classroom*, she would have said.

Dorothea swept a hand down over the ensemble, which ended just below her kneecaps. "It's just one of oodles of dresses I bought for my fall wardrobe," she said in that whiny, through-the-nose voice that always reminded Rudy of a fingernail being scraped down a chalkboard. "Father made a *killing* on the stock market this summer. It took me just *ages* to decide which one to wear this morning!"

And then she added something new to her already annoying list of mannerisms. She spread her very wide mouth and giggled.

"What was *that* sound?" Rudy said as the three of them hurried away.

"Sounded like a horse whinnyin'," Little Al said.

Hildy Helen stopped dead inside the heavy front door and peered out through the window. "She just thinks she is the snake's hips. Did you see that outfit she was wearing? I feel like a *child* in this pig's coattail!"

She looked down at her white sailor blouse with its red neck scarf and her navy blue skirt, and she scowled at the black tie-shoes and blue knee socks.

"Whatsa matter with yer outfit?" Little Al said. "I think ya look swell."

"Don't be an idiot, Little Al!" Hildy Helen said. "I look like a little school girl next to her!"

"I thought you didn't care that much about clothes and stuff anymore," Rudy said.

"It's not the clothes I care about, silly. It's just that she's going to get all the boys."

"She ain't gettin' us!" Little Al said.

"I mean the *real* boys."

Little Al looked blankly at Rudy. "What are we, chopped liver?"

"No!" Hildy Helen said, stomping her foot. "But you're my brothers. I could come to school in a feed sack and you'd never notice."

"What's a feed sack?" Little Al said.

He hadn't grown up in the country like the twins—but even Rudy wasn't quite sure what Hildy Helen was so worked up about. *Anybody*—even his own sister—was prettier than lifeless-looking, pale Dorothea with her nose reaching down to meet her chin.

"So where do we go, anyway?" Little Al said.

Rudy pointed to a crowd of kids gathered around a big bulletin board on the wall, and the three hurried to join them. Standing on her tiptoes, Hildy Helen was able to figure out that they were all craning for a glimpse of the list of their first classes.

"I'm in home economics," Hildy said. "Little Al, you're in geography, room 212, and Rudy, you have the gymnasium."

Rudy could feel himself going pale. "You mean, we aren't all in the same class?"

Hildy chuckled. "Not unless you want to be in home economics. That's cooking and sewing, Rudy."

Suddenly the building was jarred by what sounded like a fire alarm. Rudy jumped and grabbed Hildy Helen by the arm. A tall boy standing nearby, wearing a large, baggy sweater, snickered.

"What's the matter, kid?" he said in a snide voice. "Ya never heard a school bell before?"

"Not like that," Rudy said.

"Well, get used to it. It's gonna go off every hour, and when you hear it you better run, because you only got five minutes to get to your next class."

"We better get a wiggle on!" Hildy Helen said, and Rudy bolted for the nearest door.

Behind him, Sweater Boy gave a raucous laugh. "Seventh graders," Rudy heard him say. "They'll fall for anything."

Rudy forced himself to slow down and try to look casual. He hoped Sweater Boy wasn't still watching when he stopped a gray-haired woman with glasses and asked her where the gymnasium was.

He arrived there out of breath but well ahead of the next clanging of that obnoxious bell. His relief was short-lived, however, because the moment he walked through the doors and onto the varnished-to-a-shine gym floor, his path was blocked by a hulking body in gray flannel oxford bags and a white turtlenecked sweater that still smelled of the expensive department store it had obviously come from.

Rudy was ready to excuse himself for plowing into a ninth-grader when he realized he was looking into a face he knew all too well. It was the face of Maury Worthington.

There was no mistaking it, of course. It was fleshy and heavy like the rest of him, and although he was bigger and older than any other boy in the seventh grade—the consequence of having done the sixth grade three times—his features were still those of an overgrown toddler, pudgy and pink and soft. For obvious reasons,

Rudy had always resisted calling him Babyface Worthington, but it would have been just the right nickname.

It still fit him, except that since the spring Maury had added a number of pimples to his complexion, as well as a few dark hairs on his upper lip. He had also changed the style of his brownish hair, which he now wore combed straight back in a way that reminded Rudy of Picasso's head feathers.

Rudy groaned. Maury *had* been promoted to seventh grade after all, probably because Mr. Worthington was now rich as well as pushy. Even Miss Tibbs couldn't beat that.

Still, Rudy collected himself quickly. He was no match for Maury physically, being somewhat slim himself, but he did know that his one defense was his sharp wit. Maury usually thought about as quickly as a bowl of oatmeal.

"Well, if it isn't Four Eyes," Maury said.

"Yes, it is. Nice hairdo," Rudy said. "You must have used half a can of Brilliantine on that this morning."

Maury sneered. "Yeah, what's it to ya?" he said. "My old man's got stock in that company."

"Figures," Rudy said. "Something smelly and greasy."

"Oh, yeah?" Maury said, face immediately heading toward purple. "What kinda stocks your old man got? Or can he afford any?"

"Are you kidding? My father isn't stupid enough to invest his money in the stock market. Did you know half that stock's bought on borrowed money? It's all gonna come crashing down—"

"Hey!" Maury said. He took a menacing step toward Rudy. "You sayin' my old man's stupid?"

"Hey, if the shoe fits," Rudy said.

"What shoe? Hey, whatta you gettin' at?"

Rudy grinned. This was feeling good—better than anything else had lately. "Those *are* some swell kick, by the way, Maurice. Bluchers, aren't they?"

"What did you call 'em?"

"Bluchers. That's what they are—really." He could barely hold down the laughter that was bubbling up in his throat. Poor Maury thought he was being insulted even when he wasn't. Rudy thought everyone knew that bluchers were stylish, shiny shoes.

Maury reached out and curled his fingers into the front of Rudy's shirt. Pulling Rudy up to his face, he said, "Hey, Four Eyes, I just noticed somethin'."

"What's that, Maury?" Rudy said, still grinning. "Do I still have raisin toast in my teeth?"

"No." Maury's lips parted into a thick smile. "I just noticed you don't have your little protector with you."

"Who?" Rudy said.

"You know, Little Augie from Detroit. That kid that lives with you."

"Little Al?" Rudy said, and then his heart began to sink. This *was* the first time he'd had to deal with Maury without Little Al at least on the same playground. Rudy tried not to swallow. He knew that from this close Maury would be able to hear his rising fear.

A whistle pierced the air and echoed off the gym walls. "All right, everybody line up!" a harsh voice shouted. "Let's go! Turn to! This isn't grammar school anymore!"

"See you in class, Four Eyes," Maury said. And then he let go of Rudy and turned on the heels of his bluchers. Rudy followed him. Junior high school had begun.

At least Maury wasn't in his second-period English class. Little Al wasn't either, but Hildy Helen was, and Rudy slid into the seat next to hers as if he had reached an oasis on the far side of the desert.

"Don't look so happy," she whispered to him. "Dorothea's in here."

Dorothea was in the center row, right in the front, of course, smiling angelically at the teacher. Rudy didn't see how even

Dorothea could smile at *him*. He was a wiry man with salt-and-pepper hair parted straight down the middle and a mustache that reminded Rudy of a very thick toothbrush. He would have been all right, Rudy thought, if he hadn't looked as if he had a frown permanently etched into his face. The lines of his forehead were so deep, you could have stored pencils in them.

"Good morning, class," the man said when the bell had jangled. It still jarred Rudy out of his seat every time he heard it. "My name is Stanley Keating. You may call me Mr. Keating."

Rudy's nervousness began to ball itself up in his throat, and it gave him the urge to laugh out loud. He coughed slightly and chewed on his lip.

"You will hear from other students in this school that this is my first year here," Mr. Keating said as he strolled up and down, tossing a piece of chalk from one hand to the other. "That is true. It is also true that this is my first year of teaching."

Dorothea's thin arm shot up.

"Yes, miss?" Mr. Keating said.

"I just want to say," Dorothea whined, "that I think it's wonderful that a man your age had the courage to make a life change."

"Isn't she just the butterfly's boots?" Hildy Helen whispered, eyes rolling.

"Yes, well, I'm not sure courage had a great deal to do with it, Miss—" he furrowed his forehead even deeper at Dorothea.

"Just call me Dorothea," she said. "Everybody does."

"I prefer last names," Mr. Keating said, "but for now, Dorothea, I appreciate your kindness. Until this summer I owned a bookstore on Madison, but in these hard economic times, unfortunately it went out of business."

Dorothea looked down at her new Mary Janes as if she were puzzled that anyone should think these were hard economic times. Mr. Keating went on strolling and tossing the piece of chalk.

"Since books are my first love," he said, "it was only logical that I should take up teaching English. You and I, you can be sure, will be reading a number of books together this year, and since you are considered to be the brightest of the seventh grade students, I expect those books will be of a high caliber indeed."

Mr. Keating then gave a sniff that was so hard it disturbed his toothbrush of a mustache. The urge to laugh was almost more than Rudy could hold back. He chomped down harder on his lip.

"Now then," he said, "I want each of you to take out a piece of paper, and in your best penmanship, write me a one-page essay describing the event which has most changed your life. When you have completed that, please turn it in, pick up a literature text and begin reading your homework assignment, which is written on the blackboard for you."

"Forty pages of reading?" Hildy Helen said, her eyes wide as she read Mr. Keating's perfect handwriting.

Rudy barely heard her. He was staring at his piece of paper and no longer fighting back the urge to laugh. It was the urge to cry he was battling now.

The event that's changed my life? he thought. *I can't write about that. I can't write about Aunt Gussie. I'll be blubbering all over the desk!*

"I suggest you begin, Mr.—"

Rudy looked up to see Mr. Keating watching him.

"Hutchinson," Rudy said.

"Yes, Mr. Hutchinson, I suggest you begin writing if you want to keep up in this challenging class."

Rudy nodded and put his pencil to the paper. Challenging— that was what Aunt Gussie had said she hoped for for Rudy. At the thought of her sitting across the table from him at the Berghoff, telling him how bright he was, Rudy had to swallow three times to get rid of the lump in his throat.

He cleared his throat and wrote at the top of his paper *The Event That Changed My Life*. Then lining up his thoughts like a wall against his tears, he wrote, *I was actually born a rodent. You wouldn't know it to look at me now, brute that I am, but at birth the doctor held me up by my ankles and said to the nurse, "It's a chipmunk!"*

By the end of the period he had woven a tale of his miraculous transformation into a human and turned it in. He was on page five of the 40 assigned pages when Mr. Keating's shadow fell across his desk.

"I see I have found my class clown," the teacher said when Rudy looked up. "Leave the funny business to the comic strips, Mr. Hutchinson, and write this over for homework tonight, would you?"

Then he dropped Rudy's essay onto his desk top and snapped off down the aisle as if he had just scored his first classroom victory. Rudy half expected him to dust his hands together and say, "This teaching thing isn't so hard after all."

But the junior high thing was hard, that was certain. After two more classes, both of which Hildy Helen was in but not Little Al, the three of them had lunch together and mourned their fate.

"I have Dorothea in every class," Hildy Helen said. "Every class!"

"I'd rather have Dorothea than Maury," Little Al said. "I got *him* in every class, except gym."

"You should have seen the clothes *he* was wearing, Hildy Helen," Rudy said.

Little Al grunted. "Didn't make any difference. Washin' a donkey's head is a waste a water."

"Huh?" Rudy and Hildy said together.

"Old Italian sayin'. Anyway, havin' Maury in my classes ain't *that* bad, 'cause he don't know from nothin'. He makes me look smart."

Leave it to Al to look at the bright side. Rudy didn't manage to do that until activities period, which was right after lunch. They were told to go to the auditorium, where each club in the school had a table set up. They were to find the club that most interested them and join. They would meet with that club every day after lunch for 45 minutes before going on to their two afternoon classes.

Hildy Helen "got a wiggle on" for the drama club. Little Al sauntered over to the school orchestra. The lady at the table looked a little doubtful, but Rudy knew she'd change her mind as soon as she heard Little Al play the violin.

Rudy himself wandered around feeling like the bottom of a shoe. There didn't seem to be an art club, which was probably because there was an art *class*, although that was only for eighth and ninth graders. He was standing in a side aisle with his hands shoved into his pockets when a girl a couple of years older than he was said, "Hi, cutie. Did you find a club yet?"

Everything about this girl bubbled, from her voice to the frothy lace around the bottom of her polka dot dress. *Whatever club I end up in*, Rudy thought, *I hope she's not in it!*

"No," Rudy said.

"Well, jeepers! What do you like to do—you know, for funsies?"

Funsies? "Uh, I like drawing. I'm kind of an artist."

"Oh," the girl said. She frowned, and then her eyes sprang wide open. "I know! You need the Argosy Club!"

"What's Argosy?" Rudy said.

"Come on, sweetie, I'll show you!"

And with a squeal she grabbed him by the wrist and pulled him to a table which was stacked with magazines. A kid with longer-than-average hair peered out from around them and said, "You like to read?"

"Yeah, I guess," Rudy said.

"He likes to *draw*, Van," Bubbles gurgled. "Isn't that exciting?"

"Swell," said Van in a voice completely without expression. "Sit down, kid. Let's see what you can do. Muffin, you can make like an egg and beat it, all right?"

"Muffin" giggled and bubbled off to direct the next unfortunate seventh grader. Rudy sank uncertainly into the wooden folding chair Van pointed to. Van opened one of the magazines, something called *Argosy*.

"Can you draw like this?" Van said, pointing to an illustration of a bare-chested man with shaggy hair and rippling muscles sitting on the back of an elephant.

"Sure," Rudy said. "Who is it?"

Van blinked his very small, very blue eyes. "It's Tarzan, kid. You never heard of Tarzan?"

"No."

"You don't read the pulps?" Van said, tapping the stack of magazines.

This time Rudy just shook his head. Aunt Gussie wouldn't let anything but *Fortune* magazine and *The Saturday Evening Post* in the house. He didn't trust himself to be able to say that without crying. Instead, he forced a grin and said, "I don't get out that much."

"I guess not. Well, try it anyway. Here's some paper."

Van shoved a blank sheet of drawing paper and a pencil at Rudy and went back to whatever it was he was doing behind the pile of magazines. Rudy studied the illustration of Tarzan carefully. He'd never copied someone else's work before. Mostly his drawings just came out of his own head—and his own prayers. It was the way he talked to Jesus. He was pretty sure Van wouldn't be interested in that.

"Whatsa matter, kid?" Van said. "I thought you said you could draw."

"I can, but—do I have to do it exactly like this? Can I draw it my own way?"

Van shrugged. "Suit yourself," he said. And with doubt in his eyes he disappeared behind the stack again.

Rudy chewed the pencil for a second, and then he began. Before he had the first two strokes done, the auditorium noise had faded behind him, and with it Maury Worthington and Mr. Keating and classes without Little Al. The lump in his throat, the anxious feeling in his stomach, the urge to cry—it all disappeared as he drew. When he was finished, he didn't even hesitate before he tapped on the top of the magazines.

"Hey," he said. "I'm done."

"Hay is for horses, kid. The name's Va—" Van stopped in mid-word and stared at Rudy's picture. "You drew this?" he said.

"Yeah," Rudy said.

"You sure?"

Rudy snorted. "No, it was the little green men I carry in my pocket. I told you, I drew it."

"I believe ya, I believe ya." Van shook his head. "I had you for a loser, kid," he said, "but I was wrong." He looked at Rudy with his small, blue eyes. "You want to be in the club?"

"What do you do?"

"Read the pulps. Adventure stories; you'll like them. Then some of us write our own, some of us illustrate. I'm a writer myself." As if to prove it, he whipped out several hand-written pages from behind the stack and waved them toward Rudy. "You want to join?"

"Can I draw as much as I want? My way?"

"And how."

"What do I have to do?"

"Come up with a fin. That's for a subscription to *Argosy*, your dues, and the art supplies."

Rudy nodded. Five dollars shouldn't be a problem. Aunt Gussie would be happy to—

He stopped himself there and squeezed out another grin for Van. "Sign me up," he said.

And as he scribbled his name on the membership list, he thought maybe the Argosy Club was going to be the one thing that could save this school year. When he got to his last class of the day, he was sure of it.

It was woodworking, and there was Maury Worthington, seated right at his table.

"Hey, Four Eyes," he said. "I see Little Augie isn't in here either."

"Gee, Maurice," Rudy said. "You're a lot smarter than they say you are."

Although Maury was stunned into silence for a moment, Rudy felt no glow of triumph. The Argosy Club was looking better by the minute.

Chapter Four

*W*hen the three of them got home from school that afternoon, Rudy was halfway to Aunt Gussie's room to ask her for the money to join the Argosy Club when he remembered she wasn't there.

Picasso hadn't forgotten, though. He was wailing from his cage in the library: "Gustavia! Gustavia Nitz! Come see Picasso! Come see Picasso!"

"Guess I better get in there and do my job," Little Al said.

"Oh, that's right," Hildy Helen said. "We've got chores to do. I better hurry. I've got a tennis lesson at five o'clock!"

She headed off to the kitchen, and Rudy shrugged and went out to the garage, where white-haired old Sol was polishing the pink Pierce Arrow, which already had a shine a foot deep.

"I thought you waxed this thing yesterday, Sol," Rudy shouted. You had to shout at Sol. He had been getting more and more deaf since his injury last year.

"Eh?" Sol said.

"Never mind. I'm supposed to tell you where to go this afternoon."

Sol nodded vaguely.

"Take Hildy Helen to tennis lessons at five o'clock in Grant Park, then pick up LaDonna at Dad's office at five-thirty and then go back and get Hildy Helen at six o'clock. Then get Dad from his meeting at nine. You got that?"

"Eh?" Sol said.

"I *said*, 'Have you got that?'"

"Yes, sir, Mr. Rudolph."

"Aunt Gussie'll be back soon, and you can be Mr. Formal with her," Rudy said. "I'm just Rudy."

"Yes, sir, Mr. Rudolph," Sol said, and, still nodding, he climbed into the car.

Rudy had a sinking feeling as he watched the long, pink car pull away half an hour later with Hildy Helen in the backseat.

Maybe I should have gone with him, he thought.

But he brushed that away and went upstairs to practice drawing Tarzan.

When the phone rang at seven, Rudy was still drawing. He waited through several rings for Quintonia to answer it before he remembered that she was at the hospital with Aunt Gussie. The front door slammed and footsteps hurried into the library below. Rudy heard Miss Tibbs give a breathless, "Hello?"

He got downstairs just as she was hanging up. Her cheeks were flushed from rushing, and her green-gold eyes had a flustered look Rudy hadn't seen there before.

"Rudy?" she said. "Didn't you tell Sol to pick Hildy Helen up at six o'clock?"

"Yeah," Rudy said.

"Well, she's stranded at Grant Park, and it's getting dark."

"Where's LaDonna?"

"I don't know," Miss Tibbs said. "Isn't she home from work yet?"

Rudy's stomach fluttered. "I guess not, but I told Sol—"

The phone rang again. Rudy could tell from Miss Tibbs's eyes as she listened to the person on the other end that LaDonna, too, had been abandoned.

"Wait there," Miss Tibbs said to her. "We'll find Sol. Don't worry."

But she looked plenty worried herself as she replaced the candlestick phone to its holder. "What exactly did you tell Sol, Rudy?" she said.

Before he could answer, the front door slammed again, and Dad appeared in the library door.

"Dad!" Picasso cried. "Where's Gustavia? Where's Gustavia Nitz?"

"She's the only person whose location I *do* know!" Dad said. He looked more bewildered than usual.

"What are you doing here?" Miss Tibbs said. "I thought you had a meeting until nine."

"I thought I did, too, but Sol showed up and told me that Rudy said I was to come home now. I tried to call but the line was busy. Has something happened?"

"It's what hasn't happened!" Miss Tibbs said.

She looked at Rudy. "Go get Sol and go *with* him to get LaDonna and Hildy Helen."

I KNOW! Rudy thought as he shoved his way between the furniture toward the door.

"Get Gustavia Nitz!" Picasso shouted at him.

Rudy mumbled back, "I wish I could."

No one was in a very good mood when they were all finally assembled at the dinner table, except Dad who had gone back to his meeting. Hildy Helen could do nothing but complain about having to stand around at Grant Park while it got dark and spooky. LaDonna related in great detail the number of young men who had asked her to accompany them to the nearest speakeasy while she stood out on the sidewalk on Dearborn Street like a walking advertisement.

"Tomorrow, I have to be picked up exactly at five-thirty, Rudy," she said, "because I have a big test the next day, and I have to use every minute to study—or I'll never get into college or law school. In fact, I need to get upstairs right now. Will you all excuse me?"

"You didn't eat the pork chops we fixed!" Hildy Helen wailed.

LaDonna took one more stab at hers and stuffed a piece into her mouth. Her face twisted as she attempted to chew it. It *was* a little hard, Rudy thought, but he sure wasn't in a position to criticize the way anybody else did her chores.

"I have dance class tomorrow, Rudy," Hildy Helen said when LaDonna had gone out, still chomping. "Sol has to get me there by four-thirty or Miss Sappington will yell. I don't want to get thrown out of that class."

Rudy nodded.

"Did you really get that?" Hildy Helen said.

"I got that I'm a chump," Rudy said, "and that if I don't get this right LaDonna will never become a lawyer and you won't be the next Tina Ballerina or whoever it is you want to be."

Hildy Helen's face wilted. "You don't have to be so ugly about it."

"You think *you* got a hard job, Rudolpho," Little Al said. "Try babysittin' that bird. I almost went blooey listenin' to him squawk for Miss Gustavio. I hadda go out for a walk so I wouldn't wring his neck!"

"Maturity certainly has its price," Miss Tibbs said.

Three pairs of eyes glared at her. Her eyes softened. "I know this is hard, but we all have to pull together. Hildy, I think you and I need to spend a little time studying the cookbook tonight. And Little Al, let's see if we can't find some parrot books in your aunt's library that might be helpful to you. Now, Rudy—"

Rudy *really* wanted to ask her to mind her own potatoes, but Hildy Helen saved him.

"I don't have *time* to read a cookbook tonight!" she wailed. "Rudy and I have to read 40 pages for English!"

Rudy could feel himself starting to sag. Somehow if Aunt Gussie had been there, it would all have seemed so much smoother, so much easier. She would have made them feel like it could all be done. As it was, his mind was becoming more and more jumbled. He went upstairs and tried to read, and waited for Dad to come home. Only five dollars stood between him and a clear head again.

Finally the front door slammed at nine-fifteen and Rudy bounded down the stairs. He stopped short on the last landing and waited until his father and Miss Tibbs were finished hugging in the hallway and she had gone off to the kitchen to warm up his dinner.

Rudy followed his father into the library where, thankfully, Al had already covered Picasso's cage—although he was still muttering pitifully on his perch. Rudy spilled out the news about the Argosy Club before his father even got his jacket off. He practically had his hand out for the "fin" as Van had called it, when Dad began rolling up his sleeves and shook his head.

"I'm afraid I can't help you on this, son," he said.

Rudy could only stare at him.

"Sit down," Dad said, and then he sat across from Rudy on one of Aunt Gussie's leather chairs. "Things are changing around here."

"Yeah, I noticed. But how come—"

"Hear me out. The bills for your aunt's care are sky-high, and she has a long recovery ahead of her. We have to pay a registered nurse to come in at least once a day, even though Quintonia will have her full-time care. The hospital is very expensive—and the medicines. Aunt Gussie has been very wise with her money, but this will still put quite a dent in her savings." Dad shoved a weary hand through his hair. "There is more than enough for us to live on comfortably, but we have to look ahead, too. Stock market prices have been taking drops ever since September 3—"

"Aunt Gussie doesn't invest in the stock market!" Rudy said.

"No, but with the market behaving the way it is, there is going to be a financial crash. I know few people believe your aunt and me when we talk about it, but people who have really studied these things, and who are not so wrapped up in their newfound wealth that they can't see anything else, are aware that we're headed for trouble—trouble that is going to affect everyone, not just those who have money in the market."

Dad's small, dark eyes took on that faraway look they always got when he was moving into a lecture about things he strongly believed in—and which Rudy only halfway understood. He went on about business being the new religion.

"A fella told me the other day that Moses was one of the greatest salesmen and real-estate promoters that ever lived," he said.

He talked about people caring more about "tremendous trifles," like new cars and heavyweight boxing, than they did about genuine public issues like farm relief and oil scandals and the situation in Nicaragua.

Whatever that is, Rudy thought.

"We hear a lot of ballyhoo on the radio," Dad said, "while nothing is said about the economy running wild. It's as if the booming stock market has somehow made up for the decay of religious faith and the debunking of things like love and ideals. Americans are spinning wonderful dreams, but they're not about freedom from graft and crime and war. They're about prosperity and all the things it can buy—cars and planes and skyscrapers and smart clothes. They're spending their futures, Rudy, and I'm not going to spend yours."

Rudy suddenly realized they were talking about the Argosy Club again.

"If you give me five dollars, I won't have a future?" he said.

"That isn't the point, son," Dad said. "I want you to learn to respect money and develop good habits for handling it, not spend it recklessly and pursue it as if it were everything, the way people do today—"

He was going off again, and Rudy couldn't listen any longer.

"So you aren't going to give me the money?" he said.

"Not for extras like penny candy and magazines."

"But this is a club! Hildy Helen gets to have tennis lessons and dance classes!"

"There is only one more week of tennis, and both that and the dance classes have already been paid for for the term."

"I really want to join this, Dad. And we have to join at least one club for activities period!"

"Then either choose a club that doesn't require a fee, or get yourself a job after school to earn the money."

"A job?" Rudy said. "But that'll take too long. Isn't there any way I can borrow the money from you and then pay it back? I need this quick!"

Dad closed his eyes and actually shuddered. "Rudy, that is exactly the kind of thinking that has gotten people into trouble on the stock market. I want you to have a Christian work ethic, not a get-rich-quick philosophy. Now, if you are interested in finding a job, I can help you."

"No," Rudy said. "That's all right."

He said good night to Dad and walked gloomily out of the library and up the stairs. *I can't keep up with the stuff I already have to do*, he thought.

It was as if someone had just slammed the door to the room marked BE A KID and was shoving him toward the one that said GROW UP NOW.

But Dad told me not to go there, he thought.

But Dad also said to get a job.

And Aunt Gussie said not to act like a silly little kid anymore.

I don't know what I'm supposed to do! If Aunt Gussie were here, she'd explain it to me. Dad uses too many big words.

But Aunt Gussie wasn't there, and the thought of it made him angry and scared and confused, all in one big knot. He truly didn't know whether to laugh or cry.

There was only one person left to go to, and Rudy headed right for her. He found Hildy Helen lying on her bed with her feet up on the wall, her literature book held up in mid-air as she read.

"You look kinda sore," she said to him as she let the book fall to the bedspread. "What's wrong?"

He told her. She listened, nodding her shiny bob from time to time.

"If I had any money, I'd give it to you, Rudy," she said when he was finished. "You know I would."

"Yeah, I know."

"I mean, because you're my brother. And not just any brother. I mean, I love Little Al and all, but you're my twin. I'd do anything for you because we're practically the same person."

"All *right*!" Rudy said. This was getting very embarrassing.

She didn't seem to notice. "I figure that's what I have over Dorothea Worthington when it comes to boys. I *know* boys. I've lived with one since *before* I was born. She doesn't know diddly. Besides—"

She reached under the mattress and pulled out a small book which she opened to reveal some handwritten scrawling across its pages.

"Look how many boys' signatures I already have in my autograph book," she said. "I'm not stuck on any of these fellas, of course, but—well, you never know!" And then she made a sound Rudy had never heard come out of her mouth in quite that way. She tossed back her shiny head and she giggled—a high-pitched sound that went on and on like a duck on a chase.

Rudy stared from her to the autograph book and back again. If this was what they meant by growing up, it was definitely getting worse by the minute.

✛ ✛ ✛

Chapter Five

*S*omehow, Rudy got through the first week of junior high school, but at the end of it, he couldn't have explained how.

On Tuesday, the boys had to put on their gym clothes and report to the basketball court for inspection. Rudy was hurrying to get in line, still adjusting his billowing gym shorts, when a harsh voice barked, "Hutchinson! Pull up those socks!"

Rudy skidded to a halt and leaned over to give the wayward socks a tug. Something planted itself squarely in the middle of his bottom, and the next thing he knew, he was sprawled face first on the shiny floor.

The line erupted in raucous laughter and somebody said, "Hey, Worthington! You got Coach's voice down pretty good! You could go on radio!"

You could also go on the next train out of here, Rudy thought angrily. It didn't get any better when he reached for his glasses, which had popped from his face when he fell, and discovered they were so bent out of shape they wouldn't fit back on straight. He folded them up, stuffed them into his pocket, and squinted his way to the end of the line.

"Hey, Hutchinson, tie your shoe!" somebody yelled.

Rudy forced himself not to even look down and said calmly, "Hey, Worthington, there's something green and slimy coming out of your nose. Better catch that, fella. It could be part of your brains, and you can't spare any."

"Take that back, sap!" Maury shouted.

He started to lunge for Rudy, but a sharp toot from Coach's whistle held him back. Rudy smiled calmly, though his heart was pounding out the Charleston inside his chest. He'd come out ahead that day, but he still had the rest of the term to go. It didn't get any better in gym class after that.

English was almost worse. The second day, Mr. Keating assigned a book report. "It must be five paragraphs long," he said, still strolling and tossing his chalk, which made Rudy more nauseous than watching one of Hildy Helen's tennis matches. "Every word spelled correctly, no grammatical errors—that all goes without saying. Here is the key, however—"

He stopped strolling and eyed them as if he expected them all to try to make a break for the door. "I want to see your best work—the top of your form, as it were. I want to know what you're capable of. Any questions?"

Hands shot up all over the room. Dorothea's was the first, of course.

"When is this due?" she said. "I'll want to write it on my assignment pad." And then she waved a little gold pencil in the air for emphasis.

"October 24," Mr. Keating said.

Rudy let out a long, loud sigh of relief.

"I wouldn't get too comfortable, Mr. Hutchinson," Mr. Keating said. "That sounds like a long way off, but when you take into consideration the kind of book I am asking you to read, you will want to begin immediately—tonight."

"Quick, write it on your assignment pad with your little gold pencil," Hildy Helen whispered to him when Mr. Keating had turned to answer the next question.

"What kind of book?" a blond-haired boy asked.

Rudy felt Hildy Helen sit up straighter in her seat, and he glanced at her. Her brown eyes were riveted on the boy asking the question, and her lips were parted as if she were anticipating the taste of a chocolate phosphate. Rudy turned back to inspect the kid.

He had thick, wavy, straw-colored hair, and he was wearing a V-necked sweater that made him look like he ought to be in a fancy prep school in Massachusetts. He also had a set of teeth so white he should have, in Rudy's estimation, been modeling for tooth powder ads in magazines.

"Let me tell you what kind of book I do *not* have in mind," Mr. Keating was saying to Teeth. "I will not accept any Zane Grey novels, no F. Scott Fitzgerald trash—nothing of that nature. I want to see you reading the classics, things that will expand your minds."

Hildy Helen raised her hand.

"Yes, Miss Hutchinson?"

"What about Peggy Stewart books?"

Rudy thought Mr. Keating was going to lose his breakfast. "Absolutely not!" he said. "And you can forget about *Anne of Green Gables* and the like as well."

"Then what *do* you want us to read, sir?" Teeth said.

"Mr. Young, I must insist on a novel or a book of poems or even a volume of non-fiction which challenges your thinking and exposes you to quality literature, prose, or poetic language."

The entire class seemed to blink at once. Suddenly, Rudy couldn't help himself. He raised his hand.

"Yes, Mr. Hutchinson?" Mr. Keating said.

"So, I guess *Tarzan of the Apes* is out of the question?"

Mr. Keating actually gasped. Rudy fought the good fight to keep a grin off his face and won. Mr. Keating was finally able to get his breath and shake his head. "I think we all have a good idea what I am looking for," he said. "I want you to make your choice by Friday and bring the book with you to class. I will check them while you are taking your first exam."

It was the class's turn to gasp. Rudy found himself longing for Miss Tibbs.

Things became even more complicated on Wednesday when Dorothea plopped herself down at their table in the cafeteria and said, "Does anyone know where I could find Billy Young?"

"Who's Billy Young?" Little Al said.

"You mean Teeth?" Rudy said.

"Teeth?" Hildy Helen and Dorothea said in unison.

Rudy gave them the biggest toothy grin he could muster, and Dorothea let out a horrible giggle. Little Al put his hands over his ears.

"What do you want Billy for?" Hildy said. Her voice sounded tight to Rudy.

"I want him to sign my autograph book," Dorothea said.

"With your little gold pencil?" Rudy said.

"No," Hildy Helen said. "We haven't seen him."

"I seen a fella with big teeth pass by just a minute ago," Little Al said. "Does he have yella hair?"

"We *haven't* seen him," Hildy Helen said. She stared hard at Little Al, jaw clenched.

"Forget it," Little Al said to Dorothea. "We ain't seen him."

But it was too late. Dorothea had already caught sight of poor Billy and gave a squeal that set everybody at the table on their left ear. As she darted off, long beads swinging, Hildy Helen set her waxy milk carton down on the table with a thud.

"Whatsa matter?" Little Al said.

"I can't *believe* that she wants the same boy I do!" Hildy Helen said.

"Wants him for what?" Rudy said.

Hildy Helen rolled her eyes until they almost disappeared into her head. "For crying out loud!" she said.

"Oh," Little Al said to Rudy. "I think she's stuck on him."

"I bet Dorothea knows I like him. I bet that's the only reason she wants his autograph. I'd like to take those beads of hers and wrap them around her neck."

"They *are* around her neck," Little Al said.

"Tighter!" Hildy Helen looked at Rudy. "Would you help me if I asked you to do something?"

"Like what?" Rudy said. He could almost hear Aunt Gussie clicking her tongue at him.

"I don't know yet. But I just can't let her get the best of me. I just can't."

The bell rang for activities period, and Rudy then had other things to think about. It was the second day in a row he was going to have to go to Van and tell him he didn't have the money yet.

Van tossed his longish hair at Rudy that day and said, "Let me ask you this, kid. Do you have any prospects for the money?"

"Sure," Rudy lied.

"All right, then just sit here and read some stories. You gotta be somewhere. You might as well be here."

Rudy opened a copy of *Argosy* to read the latest chapter of *Tarzan at the Earth's Core*, but all he could see on the pages was the lie he'd just told. *I'm sorry, Jesus*, he thought. *I just don't know what to do about all this. You want to give me a hand here?*

He felt a little better after that. Jesus had always come through for him before, teaching him stuff, helping him along. It would be all right. Yeah.

But even after he went home that night and drew a picture of the Lord play-boxing with him, grins on both of their faces, Rudy's Jesus-confidence only lasted until LaDonna came slamming into the house at six-thirty, eyes wild.

"I could have been studying all this time!" she said to Rudy. "But no, I was *walking* from Mr. Jim's office to Hildy Helen's dance studio, where I had to convince Sol that it was Hildy Helen he was supposed to be dropping off there, not me he was supposed to be picking up."

Rudy gulped. "Where was Hildy Helen?"

"At the courthouse. Sol insisted on taking her there. He practically shoved the poor girl out of the car and wouldn't listen to her when she tried to tell him he was supposed to pick your father up there later. Rudy, are you going to straighten out this mess?"

"Yeah," Rudy said. "Sure."

But even though he talked loudly and slowly to Sol the next two afternoons with a mouth so big and exaggerated he thought it would split at the corners, the chauffeur made an even worse mess on Thursday. The only thing that made *that* day bearable was that when Rudy got home from school, Quintonia met the kids at the door and told them that Aunt Gussie was there.

"Here?" Hildy Helen said. "In this very house?"

"Hot dog!" Little Al said.

The three of them turned like a flock of herded sheep in the direction of Aunt Gussie's room, but Quintonia held up her hand.

"One at a time," she said. "And you can only stay five minutes apiece. She needs her rest."

"Let me go first, please," Rudy said.

"Sure, Rudolph," Little Al said. "I'm gonna get Picasso ready to take in there."

"I'm going to go get her some of the cookies I made yesterday," Hildy Helen said.

Rudy felt like a chump for about the thousandth time since Aunt Gussie's stroke, because he had nothing to take to her except his problems.

But at least she's better now, he told himself as he hurried to her room. *She might not be able to talk that good yet, but she won't be drooling and stuff. I mean they wouldn't have let her come home—*

His pep talk to himself stopped the minute he opened her door.

Aunt Gussie was propped up in her high bed with its square headboard from Germany. Above her head, the portraits of her parents, Austin and Sally Hutchinson, appeared to be standing guard over their little girl. Rudy realized as he padded silently across the room that she *was* like a little girl just now. It was the first time he had ever seen her in bed, and the mound of snowy white pillows all around her made her look small and fragile, something Aunt Gussie never was.

As Rudy got closer, he saw that the left side of her face was still slack-looking, but she had a handkerchief clutched in her right hand, and she dabbed at the left corner of her mouth before she looked at Rudy out of only one eye. The other one remained closed.

It was a disturbing sight, but Rudy forced himself to grin at her. "Am I glad to see you, Aunt Gussie!" he said. "And how! It's been awful without you. I can't even tell you how much I hate junior high. You said you wanted me to be challenged, but there's a difference between being challenged and being stood up in front of a firing squad, if you ask me! Do you know a fella named Stanley Keating? He's our English teacher. I thought you might know him because he used to own a bookstore before it went broke and he became a teacher. I wish you'd buy his bookstore back for him so he could go back to it."

Aunt Gussie held up her right hand, still holding the hanky, and Rudy took a breath.

"Sorry," he said. "I guess I oughta let you get a word in edgewise."

He stood and waited. Aunt Gussie drew up the right side of her face and twisted her mouth, but for a moment nothing came out. Rudy leaned forward and nodded, as if that were going to help her. She let out a moan.

"Yeah?" Rudy said.

But she shook her head, and her tongue fumbled its way out to lick her lips, and then she twisted her face again. This time two moans came out. Rudy kept nodding, but Aunt Gussie shook her head hard and slapped at the bed covers with her right hand.

"Just keep trying, Aunt Gussie," Rudy said. "You'll get it out."

Aunt Gussie waggled her finger at him, forcing more moans from her misshapen mouth, until her hand dropped and she let her head fall back onto the pillows.

"Rest a second," Rudy said. "You almost had it that time."

But Aunt Gussie shook her head once more. She was breathing hard, and she raised her right arm one more time, this time to point to the door.

"You want me to get Quintonia?" Rudy said.

She shook her head and pointed again. Then she pointed to Rudy and back at the door.

"You want me to go?" Rudy said.

She nodded and closed her eyes. When she wouldn't look at him again, he left the room.

Little Al met him in the hall with Picasso on his shoulder. "Is she ready for me?" he said.

"I don't know," Rudy said miserably. Then he went upstairs and drew a picture of himself and Aunt Gussie, gags in their mouths, looking around with searching eyes. *Where are You, Jesus?* he prayed. *Are You gonna tell me what to do now?*

Maybe I'm already supposed to know, he thought. *Maybe that was why Aunt Gussie got disgusted and threw me out. Maybe God doesn't answer prayers about stuff we could fix ourselves.*

That was an even more depressing thought. He decided not to even go downstairs for dinner, and LaDonna came up to get him. She found him lying on his stomach on the bed, drawing cartoons of Maury Worthington in his sister's clothes.

"You're in a bad way," LaDonna said, looking over his shoulder.

"If you came in here to yell at me, you might as well save your breath," Rudy said.

"What good would it do me?" she said. "I've decided to try bribing you into getting it right with Sol."

Rudy looked at her sharply. "You mean, give me money? Like five dollars?"

LaDonna gave a lady-like sniff. "No, I'm saving all my money for college, boy. I mean, I could help you with a homework assignment or something."

"Write my book report for me," Rudy said glumly.

A thinly penciled eyebrow shot up. "I'm not going to write it for you. Miss Gussie would have my head if I did that. But I will help you. What book are you reading?"

"I don't know."

"That's a good start."

"I'm a chump."

"You're feeling sorry for yourself is what you are. I'll bring you a book after supper. Right now, you'd better get downstairs. Quintonia is back, and she doesn't stand for anybody missing a meal."

"Did Hildy Helen cook it?"

"She helped."

"Do you have any digestive tablets?"

LaDonna smiled. "Come on. We're all in this together."

Later that night, Rudy found a book on his bed. *God's Trombones,* the cover said. *Poems by James Weldon Johnson.*

Rudy flipped through and looked at some of the titles. "The Creation," "The Prodigal Son," and "Noah Built the Ark."

"You don't get much older than this," Rudy said to Hildy Helen, who was reading her own book. "At least I got a book to show Mr. Keating tomorrow. What are you taking in?"

Hildy gave a long, dreamy sigh. "LaDonna gave me a romance. *Jane Eyre.*"

"A romance?" Little Al said. "Sounds sappy."

"Well, so far it isn't. She's an orphan, and she's having to fight like the dickens to hold her own."

"Oh," Little Al said. "I like a doll like that."

So, apparently, did Mr. Keating, because he approved her selection right away. He frowned at Rudy's for a while, and Rudy started wondering if he stuck his finger between the furrows of the man's brow if it would cut off his blood circulation. Finally, Mr. Keating nodded and handed the book back to Rudy.

"All right," he said, "we'll see what you can do with that. But no fooling around, Mr. Hutchinson."

"None, sir," Rudy said.

"I mean it. If I see anything clownish in this report, I will give you an F, no questions asked."

Rudy felt his face going red.

"This is no laughing matter, Mr. Hutchinson!"

"I wasn't laughing, sir!"

"Really? Then what is that twinkle that is constantly in your eyes—as if you are always enjoying some secret joke the rest of us are not privy to?"

"I'll try to get rid of it, sir," Rudy said.

"Oh, go sit down, Mr. Hutchinson!" And Mr. Keating waved him off as if he were shooing away a fly.

At activities period that day, Van got the club going full swing. "We're going to read a story by Horace McCoy out loud," he said. "Then you can either draw or write what it inspires." He looked at Rudy. "I hope you have some prospects for your dues, kid," he said, "because I can't wait to see what you come up with."

"Why?" another boy said.

"Because the kid here is good. Real good. I want to use some of his stuff."

"For what?" Rudy said.

"For our own magazine we put out," Van said. "But you gotta belong to the club—pay your dues, all that stuff—before you can contribute."

Then a girl started reading out loud. Rudy listened and decided that tomorrow he was going to go get a job.

✛ ⚫✛⚫ ✛

Chapter Six

As he'd promised he would, Dad helped Rudy out with the job situation. He sent him down to Randolph Street, not far from his own office, to a bakery owned by one of his former clients.

"Here's a note for Oscar," Dad said. "Go on your bicycle, and he'll probably hire you to make deliveries for him."

Rudy's spirits lifted as he rode his bike through the city. It was a crisp September Saturday, just on the warm side of cool, and as he wove in and out among the cars, he could enjoy Chicago. It was hard to decide sometimes which was his favorite of the city's buildings— the white Wrigley Building that shimmered in the sun, the Tribune Tower that looked like a sand castle at the top, or the Chicago Water Tower that proudly reminded everyone it had survived the great fire of 1871. It was a wonderful place to live, Chicago, because you could always hear jazz and you could always smell food.

Rudy could definitely smell food as he parked his bike in front of the Randolph Street Bakery. The aromas of fresh bread and sugar cookies wafted out of the open door, and Rudy wondered if he could take part of his pay in treats.

No, he told himself firmly. *I have to save it all for the Argosy Club.*

He straightened his shoulders and put on his best grin and went in.

A short man with thick gray hair was standing behind the counter in a white apron. Rudy at once liked the expression on his face. He didn't appear to be looking at anything in particular, but he seemed amused, as if life itself made him want to chuckle. Rudy felt himself relax as he stepped up to the counter.

"I'm Rudy," he said, digging in his pocket for his father's note. "I'm looking for a job as a delivery boy."

"Are you now?" the man said. He still looked amused.

Rudy paused with the note in his hand. "Are you Oscar?"

"How did you know?"

"My father sent me." He gave Oscar Dad's letter and looked around while he read it. It was a small bakery, but sparkling clean and stuffed with every kind of delicacy Rudy could have dreamed up and then some. Quintonia was a great cook, but she was always so concerned about the children getting all their vitamins, she had to be wheedled into making eclairs and cream puffs and some of the other goodies Rudy found himself drooling over at the moment. He had stepped even closer to the counter to examine a particularly delicious-looking raspberry scone when he heard someone say, "Pop! You aren't going to hire *him*?"

Rudy's head snapped up and he found himself looking into a pair of eyes that couldn't seem to decide whether to be green or blue. The freckled-nose face looked familiar, though he couldn't place it, but its owner seemed to be having no trouble identifying him.

"You know this boy?" Oscar said.

"We met," the blonde girl said. "When I was still working at the Berghoff before school started. I caught him pouring salt into some poor woman's sugar bowl."

She fell into place in Rudy's head with a thud. The waitress at the restaurant that day he was in there with Aunt Gussie. The same day she—

Rudy cleared his throat. "Aunt Gussie and I always clowned around like that," he said. "She knew I was just kidding with her."

Ingrid looked at Oscar. "Does that sound like a harmless little prank to you, Pop? Do you want this little urchin putting salt on our customers' doughnuts?"

Oscar frowned slightly at the note Rudy had given him, but his face softened at once back into its expression of amusement. "No son of Jim Hutchinson's would do a thing like that!" he said. "How often can you work, liebschen?"

"Every day after school and on Saturdays," Rudy said. "I can't work Sundays. We always go to church."

"Lutheran?" Oscar said.

"Presbyterian."

"Not so bad! All right then. For those hours, I'll give you 50 cents a week and one snack a day."

Rudy made a quick calculation in his head. At that rate, it was going to take him 10 weeks to earn enough to get into the Argosy Club. He cleared his throat again. "If I don't take any snacks, can we make it a dollar a week?"

"Seventy-five cents. That's my final offer."

"Pop!" Ingrid cried.

"It's a deal," Rudy said.

Oscar's face grew even more amused, and he stuck out his hand across the counter. Rudy shook it, grinning back at him.

"You're going to be sorry," Ingrid said. "But then, that's just my opinion."

"That's enough out of you, Inky," Oscar said. "Introduce him to your mother, and then give him his list for the afternoon. He can start right away."

Rudy's heart sank a little. Ingrid was going to be giving the orders? This could be tough.

But he liked Oscar's wife, Sylvia Feilchenfeld, who was a gray version of Ingrid, except that she never stopped smiling. Ingrid, it seemed, never started.

"Seventy-five cents," Ingrid muttered as she drew up a list for Rudy. "I'd better not catch you taking any snacks, or I'll fire you myself."

Rudy immediately stopped sniffing the air and made up his mind never to give this girl the satisfaction.

Ingrid stood up and handed him the list and a box that was bursting with the sweet smell of frosting.

"Can you carry this on your handlebars?" she said.

Rudy nodded.

"Deliver everything in here by five o'clock. That's when we close on Saturdays. Anything falls on the pavement, you pay for it out of your wages. Do you know your way around the city?"

"I've lived here a year."

"That's not long enough, if you want my opinion, but nobody seems to today. Let me point out that I've listed your deliveries in order, the things that need to stay hot being delivered first. Don't stray from this list or we'll get complaints, and then you'll get the ax. Got it?"

Nice girl, Rudy thought as he loaded the box onto his handlebars and took off down Randolph Street. *But that's all right. I'm gonna show her.*

But showing her was a lot harder than it sounded.

In the first place, there were streets in Chicago that Rudy had never heard of. He got lost three times in the first hour.

The clocks on the corner seemed to be shouting at him, "Hurry up! This stuff is getting cold!" every time he rode past them, which he seemed to be doing at an alarming rate. He kept looking over his shoulder to make sure the motorcycle police weren't after him.

There were scones to be delivered to an apartment above the

dress shop on Washington. Then a half dozen doughnuts to be taken all the way down to Harrison. Then one lone eclair to a man who was in the observation tower at the top of the Wrigley Building. The man popped in his dentures, scolded Rudy for making him wait so long, then had the thing devoured before Rudy could get to the elevator.

There were 18 items to deliver in all, and Rudy somehow got each one to its destination before the corner clocks shouted 4:45. One cupcake did take a tumble to the sidewalk on LaSalle just before his last delivery, but Rudy dusted it off, stuck it back in the box, and wheeled on, hoping nobody had seen him.

Sorry, Jesus, he prayed. *But I really, really need this money.*

By the time he was headed back to Randolph Street, Rudy's legs ached from pedaling his bike. His eyes burned from the smoke that poured out of the factory stacks. His ears were ringing from the city's screaming sirens and honking horns and hammering construction workers. By then, the jazz all sounded mournfully sad, his favorite buildings were glaring down at him from a million eyes, and his mouth no longer watered for anything, much less something that had come out of that empty box on his handlebars.

When he reached the bakery, Rudy plastered a smile on his face, straightened his shoulders once more and marched inside holding the box with one hand over his shoulder.

"There you are, madam," he said to Ingrid. "The job's done."

Ingrid glanced up at the clock and then back at Rudy's face. Slowly, a smile began to dawn on it.

Got her! Rudy thought.

But Ingrid folded her arms across her chest, and the smile hardened. "Just as I thought, Hutchinson," she said. "You've never worked a day in your life, have you?"

Rudy hoped he didn't look as stunned as he felt. He forced his grin to stay on his face. "Now I have," he said.

She just grunted and said, "We'll see if you even come back on

Monday."

Rudy did—and Tuesday. By Wednesday, he had blisters on his hands from his bicycle and a bruise on his tailbone from perching on the seat. All he could think about on the way home in the almost-dark was climbing into the bathtub. He didn't even want dinner, especially if Hildy Helen had a hand in it. She and Miss Tibbs, it turned out, did not make the best team in the kitchen, even with Quintonia's help.

But Rudy's dream of a bath and bed was not to be. There was a black, boxy police car parked out front on Prairie Avenue, and when he walked in the front door, voices drifted from the dining room.

"It's our working boy!" Dad called out. "Come in here, Rudy!"

With visions of hot, steamy water still in his head, Rudy went for the dining room. Everyone was there, except Aunt Gussie, of course, including two visitors. One he knew was Detective Zorn, their policeman friend. The other was a stranger.

"Eliot Ness," Dad said, "I would like for you to meet my son Rudolph. Rudy, this is Mr. Ness. He's the special agent for the federal government I was telling you about."

"He's here to get the goods on Al Capone," Little Al said. "And Mr. Hutchie's just the man to give 'em to him."

Mr. Ness just nodded as he stood up to offer his hand to Rudy. He had a quiet look about him. He must have been as handsome as Billy Young, the way Hildy Helen was gaping at him, but Rudy just liked the warm way he shook his hand. It had been a long, ugly day, and his unspoken respect almost made Rudy want to cry.

"I've heard a lot about you from Detective Zorn," Mr. Ness said as he settled himself back in front of a plate of dubious looking vegetables. "He says you're a fine young man."

"Thanks," Rudy said. He shrugged and smiled shyly at Detective Zorn's watchful eyes and then studied his supper. If those were green beans, they were the most shriveled-up version he'd ever seen.

"They're from a frozen package," Hildy Helen whispered to him excitedly. "It's the latest thing."

"What'll they think of next?" Rudy muttered back.

"I'm glad your whole family is here now, Jim," Mr. Ness said. "I think it's important for all of them to know what you're up against."

"You're talkin' about threats from the Mob if Mr. Hutchie sings," Little Al said.

"Sings?" said Miss Tibbs.

"He means if I testify against them," Dad said. "We've had threats before."

"We've had worse than threats!" LaDonna began to count off on her long, slim fingers. "The children have been kidnapped. Sol has nearly lost his hearing from being beaten up. Miss Gussie and Mr. Jim were framed as communists. Should I go on?"

"But you're all still alive," said Mr. Ness in his quiet voice. "They could change that very quickly. We've made progress with the Capone outfit. I'm sure you know that this last January we staged a raid on Chicago Heights and took over all their breweries, their speakeasies, and their gambling establishments."

"That's where Mr. Ness here and his buddies got the name the 'Untouchables'," Little Al said to Rudy. It was apparent Little Al had found a new role model to replace Al Capone himself.

"That didn't scare Capone much, though," Detective Zorn put in, his voice crisp and matter-of-fact as always.

"Exactly my point. In fact, I think it only made him mad. It's like shaking a stick at a rattlesnake. Worse, because that $100-million-a-year criminal empire of his is the single most powerful force in this city."

"I'm much more concerned about the economy than I am about the Mob at this point," Dad said. "As you've said, you've made progress with Capone in a sense. We're making none in convincing people to stop speculating on the market. It was back up again today, and I understand people rushed to buy like a bunch of starving dogs going after a bone."

Speaking of starving, Rudy thought, looking ruefully at his plate. An English mutton chop lay shriveled and slightly blackened on the china, and his stomach rumbled. Miss Tibbs and Hildy Helen had obviously cooked dinner again.

"But it isn't just you we're concerned about, Jim," Detective Zorn said. "What about your family? You know they won't hesitate to try to take your kids—"

A vague smile crossed Dad's face. "Are you trying to talk me *into* or *out of* helping you?"

"Of course we want your help," Mr. Ness said. "But I want to make sure you know that this is a man who has probably been responsible for 500 murders in this decade and hasn't been convicted of a single one because his organization has bribed almost every police officer and judge and jury in Chicago."

"And no one has dared to step in and stop him," Dad said.

"Mr. Hutchie ain't afraid a nothin'!" Little Al said. "And the rest of us Hutchies, we're just like him!"

Dad shook his head. "I don't know about that. But I do know this—and it's something my aunt reminded me of—one of the last things she said to me before she lost her ability to speak. It's a verse from Isaiah, actually. Goes something like, 'Truth faileth, and he that departeth from evil maketh himself a prey.' But, and here's the most important part: 'The Lord saw it, and it displeased him that there was no judgment.' I think the people in this city are about fed up with it, too." Dad looked down at his plate, then back up again. "Rudy," he said.

Rudy looked up from what he'd finally figured out must be fried potatoes.

"I'm going to give you another job," Dad said. "Whenever I'm not here, would you please be responsible for seeing that all the doors and windows are securely locked?"

"And I'll help him," Hildy Helen said brightly. "I won't even open the door to a salesman." Her eyes were sparkling at Mr. Ness.

But Rudy's eyes weren't sparkling. In fact, he thought if he didn't get out of this room, they were going to pop from his head.

Another job? he thought. *One more thing to be responsible for?*

He couldn't do it. He knew he couldn't do it—unless something else gave somewhere. And that couldn't be his job at the bakery or his scheduling of Sol or his schoolwork. What could he possibly do to take the pressure off all this?

He didn't get his answer until the next day.

They were in English class, waiting for the bell to ring and for Mr. Keating to arrive, when Dorothea waltzed in, pale eyes showing the first real sign of life Rudy had ever seen in them. She dropped into her desk, held a piece of folded paper to her chest, and sighed dramatically.

"What's the matter, Dorothea?" Hildy Helen said dryly. "Having an asthma attack?"

Dorothea looked around carefully and then leaned from her desk toward the twins. "You'll never guess who this note is from," she said. She produced the piece of paper, which was folded up like a flattened cone.

"Uh, the Farm League," Hildy Helen said. "They want you to be a scarecrow for their next convention."

"No, it's from the theater," Rudy said. "They're doing 'Jack and the Beanstalk,' and they want you to be the beanstalk."

Dorothea scowled at them. "You're both so mean. I don't think I'll tell you after all."

"Oh, come on, Dorothea," Hildy Helen said. "You know you want to. Who's the note from?"

Dorothea didn't hesitate for more than two seconds. "It's a love note," she said, wiggling her colorless eyebrows. "And it's from

Billy Young."

Billy Young himself chose that moment to come in the door, and Dorothea resumed a position of coy innocence in her desk, tucking the note carefully into the top of her dress. Rudy turned to roll his eyes at Hildy Helen, but he stopped when he saw the tears forming in hers.

"Oh, come on," he whispered to her. "What's that to you?"

"I like Billy Young," she whispered back. "And I despise Dorothea! She takes everything I want, just because I want it!"

Hildy Helen flounced herself toward the window, where Rudy knew she was blinking back her tears and straightening her face. Rudy looked at Dorothea, who was alternating between directing smug looks at Hildy Helen and sultry ones at Billy Young. That was when it hit Rudy: There was something that could put a hole in his pressure cooker of a life and keep him from feeling like he was going to explode any minute.

"Hey, Hildy," he whispered. "You want to have some fun with Dorothea?"

Her eyes lit up, and Rudy began to lick his lips.

Chapter Seven

*T*he fun began that afternoon at the bakery. Rudy raced through his deliveries so that the last one, a batch of petits fours for someone's dinner party, was delivered by four o'clock, and he was back on Randolph Street when Sylvia was still decorating a birthday cake.

She was standing at a table in the window as she often did to attract the attention of passersby. Sylvia, Rudy had discovered, seldom talked, but she liked to perform for possible customers.

Rudy dumped off his empty box with Ingrid and made a beeline for the front window.

"You sure are good at that," Rudy said, perching himself on a tall stool beside Sylvia.

"I try," she said. And then, of course, she smiled. Rudy had often wondered if she grinned in her sleep.

"Is it hard?" he said.

"No."

"You make it *look* easy," Rudy said. "But it looks so swell when you're done, I bet it's hard. You're just being modest."

Sylvia's eyes shone. "You want to try it?" she said.

"Me?" Rudy almost felt guilty as he opened his eyes wide and pointed to his chest. But he had Hildy Helen to think of—and the fun they were going to have, finally.

"Here. Try," Sylvia said.

As he took the paper cone from her and pointed it at the naked hunk of discarded cake she pushed toward him, Rudy was careful to note how much frosting was stuffed into the cone and how the paper was folded. Yes, this was going to be so perfect.

"Now squeeze," Sylvia said.

Rudy did, and frosting spurted out across the table.

"Not that hard," Sylvia said, smiling even bigger.

"Let me try again," Rudy said. But he had already seen what he needed to see.

After covering the hunk of cake with curlicues and swirls, Rudy asked Sylvia if he could take a cone and some frosting home to practice with. Sylvia was delighted and was humming through her smile as she carried the bowl back to the kitchen to clean up.

Ingrid, however, was neither smiling nor humming. She was standing in the doorway, frowning at Rudy.

"What are you up to, Hutchinson?" she said.

Rudy tried his innocent, "Me?" but it didn't fly with Ingrid. She watched with her blue-green eyes in slits as Rudy carefully wrapped the icing cone in waxed paper and tucked it into his jacket pocket.

"I know you could care less about decorating cakes. You'd just better not be playing my mother for a fool is all. My folks have been good to you, better than you deserve, and I won't have you using them. And another thing—"

But the bell on the door jangled, and Ingrid and Rudy both put on their customer faces. Rudy's froze when he saw that it was LaDonna coming into the bakery.

"Can I help you?" Ingrid said.

"No, thanks," LaDonna said. "But he can."

She pointed a manicured finger at Rudy, who groaned.

"Don't tell me," he said. "Sol didn't pick you up."

"No, and he didn't pick me up yesterday either, but I took the bus. I don't have any money with me today so you, cousin dear, are going to take me home on the back of your bicycle."

"You're just razzing him, right?" Ingrid said. "You aren't really going to trust him to get you home in one piece."

LaDonna smiled at her and put out her hand. "You're a girl after my own heart. LaDonna Hutchinson."

"Ingrid Feilchenfeld." She appraised LaDonna with her eyes. "You have to be related somehow. Why else would you be seen in public with this character?"

"He's my cousin," LaDonna said. "In a roundabout way. Long story."

"I'd love to hear it some time. So you're a working girl, too?"

"I work for Rudy's father in his law office."

"No offense, but isn't it a little unusual, a lawyer having a Negro secretary?"

"Not for Mr. Jim. I'll tell you the kind of man he is. He won't even let anybody go in and out the back door of the building. He wants everybody using the front door because everybody is equal—"

Rudy stood there staring as the two young women leaned on the counter and settled into a conversation as if they were at a ladies' tea.

Pretty soon there isn't gonna be anybody on my side, he thought. The icing cone in his pocket was looking better all the time.

"I'm planning to go to college, too," Ingrid was saying. "And not just to find a husband. That's what my friends accuse me of."

"They don't know what they're talking about," LaDonna said. "Who would go through all those entrance exams just to hook some man?"

"And how! Have you started studying for them yet?"

LaDonna shook her head. "On top of everything else, who has

the time?"

Rudy stirred restlessly. He wanted to get home and show Hildy Helen what he had for her.

"My chariot awaits," LaDonna said to Ingrid. "I'd love to talk again some time."

"You know it," Ingrid said. "Come by anytime."

LaDonna looked at Rudy. "I hope this'll be the last time I have to come by for *this* reason."

"I wouldn't count on it."

Ingrid gave Rudy one more stony look before they left.

Rudy did manage to wobble home with LaDonna sitting sidesaddle on the back of his bike, and to get to Hildy Helen in the kitchen to show her the icing cone before he—or it—burst. She loved it.

"I can't *wait* until tomorrow," she said.

Miss Tibbs came in from the pantry then with two sacks and wanted to know which was flour and which was cornstarch. Rudy tucked the cone away and exchanged winks with Hildy Helen.

By the next day before English class, when Hildy Helen and Rudy met in the hall outside the room, the icing cone had been tucked into another piece of paper, tightly folded into the shape Billy Young seemed to be fond of. It was going to take a good tug, and hopefully a tight hold, to get it open.

"You sure this is going to work?" Hildy Helen said.

"We tried it eight times last night!" Rudy said. "And the way we have it in there, she's gonna have to hold it really tight to get the 'note' out. One good squeeze, and blammo!"

"I know. I just really want to see her get it."

"Shhh!" Rudy said. "Here she comes."

Dorothea was sidling down the hall toward them, dressed from head to toe in a plaid that was so large it seemed to wear *her*. She looked casually over her shoulder every few feet.

"Looking for someone, Dorothea?" Hildy Helen said.

Dorothea's eyes narrowed. "I wouldn't tell you if I was," she said.

"That's too bad," Hildy Helen said, "because somebody told me *he* was looking for *you*."

"Who?" Dorothea said.

"Billy Young." Rudy could tell Hildy Helen could barely contain herself now. "He asked me to give you this."

She held out the "note," and Rudy held his breath.

But there was no need. Dorothea snatched it from Hildy and eyed it so hungrily, Rudy was sure she knew that what was inside was edible.

He could feel Hildy Helen pinching him on the arm as Dorothea made a move to pry open her treasure.

And then the unbelievable happened. Mr. Keating strode around the corner at that very moment and said, "The bell is going to ring, ladies and gentlemen. Into the classroom or it's after school for all of you."

Dorothea put the "note" behind her back and darted obediently into the room. Hildy Helen dragged at Rudy's arm.

"You don't think she'll open it in *there*, do you?" she said.

"Nah. Not with Mr. Keating ready to jump on anybody who breathes too loud."

"But I wanted to see her do it!"

"You'll see it. We'll follow her after class—"

Mr. Keating came back out to close the door, and the twins dashed in, hitting their seats just as the bell rang.

Mr. Keating called the roll. Students busied themselves sharpening pencils and assembling paper and books. Hildy Helen and Rudy watched Dorothea.

"Look at her, Rudy," Hildy Helen whispered. "It's driving her nuts!"

Rudy craned his neck to get a glimpse of the note in Dorothea's lap. She wrapped her skinny fingers around it, pulled her hand away and touched it again. All the while, she continually glanced over her shoulder at Billy Young, who was toying with a coin, unaware of the attention he was getting.

"Oh, no," Hildy Helen suddenly hissed.

Rudy's head snapped back toward Dorothea just in time to see her slowly sneaking the "note" from her lap to the desktop. She was keeping her eyes glued to Mr. Keating, who was only down to "Foster" on the roll as he meticulously pronounced each name.

"She wouldn't," Rudy whispered to his sister.

"Oh—my—gosh, Rudy! There she goes—"

Hildy's voice squeaked out as Dorothea could stand it no longer. Grasping the paper tightly on one end, she pulled open what she thought was a love letter from Billy Young. Before it was halfway apart, her face was splattered with pink frosting.

One large glob hung precariously from her hooked nose like fish bait as Dorothea let out a shriek. But it was no match for the squeals and guffaws that came from the rest of the class as one by one they saw Dorothea looking like an accident in a cake decorating class. Even Mr. Keating let out a bleat when he saw her, though *his* silenced all the rest.

"What in the name of heaven?" he said.

Dorothea opened her mouth to answer. The glob on her nose came loose and dropped right in. As panicked as he was, Rudy could no longer hold back. He muffled his face in his hands and snorted into his palms.

"Miss Worthington!" Mr. Keating said, mustache quivering. "You know I do not allow food in this classroom!"

"I didn't bring it. It was given to me!"

"By whom?"

Hildy Helen pinched Rudy's arm again.

Dorothea turned toward them. Rudy had to choke back the biggest laugh yet. He fell into a coughing fit that brought tears to his eyes.

Meanwhile, Dorothea was whipping her speckled face away from them toward the unsuspecting Billy Young and then back again.

"Well?" Mr. Keating said. "Who gave you this?"

But Dorothea was so muddled, all she could do was drop her face to the desktop and cry. Hildy Helen dropped hers and silently laughed.

"Oh, for crying out loud," Mr. Keating said. "Miss Hutchinson!"

Hildy Helen's head snapped up, and her laughter died on her lips. Rudy froze.

"Yes, sir?" Hildy Helen said.

"Would you please accompany Miss Worthington to the washroom?"

Rudy wanted to melt into a puddle. Hildy Helen scrambled up and disappeared out the door behind a sobbing Dorothea. Rudy was still trying to keep himself from letting out a giveaway sigh of relief, when he caught Mr. Keating watching him. Mr. Keating's forehead furrowed into crevices as their eyes met. Rudy tried not to cringe, even though Mr. Keating was boring holes into *his* forehead with his glare.

He knows, Rudy thought.

He could feel droplets of perspiration popping out on his upper lip, and he was close to throwing himself on the mercy of the court when Mr. Keating narrowed his eyes, stroked his mustache, and went back to the roll call.

But how could he know? Rudy thought. *Not a chance! He doesn't have the goods on me!*

But Hildy Helen didn't fare as well in the washroom with Dorothea.

"She said, 'Just wait until my brother gets ahold of you!'" Hildy Helen told Rudy after class.

"What's he gonna do, take away my ballet slippers?" Rudy said. He was feeling rather smug by then. "Besides, it was worth it, wasn't it, to see Dorothea get what she had coming?"

"It *was*, wasn't it? And the best part was Billy Young's face. Did you see how hard he was laughing? Thanks for helping me, Rudy."

But Rudy didn't need any thanks. He was feeling better than he'd felt since—well, for a while now. A grin came to his face that stayed there.

At least it stayed until woodshop class. Rudy went to the sawhorse to cut a piece of wood for the shelf he was making. He had just placed the plank carefully across the sawhorse and was reaching for the hand saw, when a blade magically appeared right next to Rudy's hand. Another hand came down on Rudy's wrist and held it in place.

"My turn, Hutchinson," Maury said near Rudy's ear. "Where do you want it cut?"

Rudy faked a snicker. "Right across the fingers there, Maurice. That oughta do it."

"I *will* do it," Maury said. And indeed he edged the blade so close to Rudy's fingers, the hairs below his knuckles stood up. Rudy swallowed painfully.

"I will," Maury said. The blade touched skin, and then it was gone. "If you don't leave my sister alone, I *will* do it."

And then he moved away.

After five minutes, Rudy finally breathed. He'd forgotten the close calls you had when you gave people the business. But when his heart slowed down to its normal rate and his palms stopped sweating, he grinned again. It was worth it, just knowing there was some way to keep from feeling as if his world were going to make him explode any minute. It was worth it, just to feel like a kid once more.

-✞- -✞- -✞-

Chapter Eight

*I*t was hard to hang onto the feeling he got from the icing caper. It seemed as if something were always happening to put the pressure on again.

Mr. Keating piling on homework and constantly reminding them about their book reports which loomed on the horizon like a tidal wave.

Sol promising that he finally had the schedule right, and then leaving Hildy Helen to hoof it home from dance class three afternoons in a row.

Aunt Gussie moaning for Quintonia to come to her room—and Quintonia telling Rudy not to even consider going near her. "She gets too upset," Quintonia would say and then snap the door shut behind her.

Rudy did get one lift the next Friday. Oscar presented him with $1.50 for two weeks' work.

Only $3.50 more to go, Rudy thought happily as he tucked the money safely into the pocket of his knickers.

But his glow faded the minute LaDonna showed up.

"Not again," he said.

"Again," LaDonna said. "Sorry, Ingrid. We'll have to walk with your pal, here."

"I can handle him," Ingrid said. She pulled off her apron and reached for a sweater hanging on the coat rack.

"What's she talking about?" Rudy said.

"She'll be going home with us," LaDonna said. "We're going to study for the college entrance exams together."

"I want to meet your father, Hutchinson," Ingrid said. "I want to give him my condolences."

Rudy didn't know what a condolence was, but he was sure he didn't want his father to have one—or anything else that came from Ingrid. Maybe he could get her to turn around and go back before they got to Prairie Avenue.

But even though he brought out his best teasing as he trudged beside the two girls, walking his bike, Ingrid was his match.

"So, what are you gonna study in college, Inky?" he said. "How to make smart cookies?"

"You really slaughter me with your wit, Hutchinson. And no, I don't need to *make* smart cookies. I *am* a smart cookie. Oh, and only my father calls me Inky. Anybody else who tries it gets a *punch* in the nose."

"What *are* you going to study?" LaDonna said.

Rudy was suddenly elbowed out of the conversation and could only listen as they spun their dreams of living on their own.

"I'm going to live in some sweet little place with bright wallpaper," LaDonna said.

"You can get a nice 12-by-12 room for $5 a week," Ingrid said.

Rudy's thoughts drifted from the conversation, then back again.

"No class rushes and pajama parades for me," LaDonna said.

"I'm going to be at the top of my class," Ingrid said.

Rudy shook his head and mumbled his disagreement.

"George Washington Carver founded the Tuskegee Institute, but he couldn't even get served in a white restaurant, and I'm going to put a stop to that kind of discrimination," LaDonna said.

"The whole German culture vanished from America because of the war, and I'm going to bring it back," Ingrid said.

"What are you going to do?" Rudy said, shouldering his way back in. "Make them serve bratwurst and sauerkraut in the school cafeterias?"

"The Germans are the biggest immigrant population in Chicago, Hutchinson," Ingrid said. "It could happen."

LaDonna nudged Rudy with her elbow. "It would have to be better than what Miss Tibbs and Hildy Helen serve, right?"

That was true, but it didn't do much to improve Rudy's mood. It was bad enough having to put up with Ingrid's evil eye at work. Now he was going to have it at home, too. He ignored the rest of their conversation and began to devise a plan to make sure it didn't ever happen again.

She'll never want to come back once I'm through, he told himself.

When they finally got home, Rudy went straight to the kitchen to find Hildy Helen. His heart sank when Miss Tibbs told him Sol had just left to pick her up.

"I don't understand why he can't get this straight," Miss Tibbs said. "I know you're talking loud enough to him. I can hear you shouting in the garage all the way from here."

Rudy grunted and started to leave the kitchen, but Miss Tibbs stopped him.

"I need to talk to you, Rudy," she said. "Sit down."

Rudy dropped into a chair and looked around for something to occupy him while she "talked." He could always make faces at himself in the glass cabinet fronts.

"And listen carefully," she said.

Miss Tibbs sat at the table, too, and folded her hands in her lap. Her green-gold eyes locked onto his and wouldn't let go. So much for making faces.

"I want to tell you about something that happened today," she said. "All the teachers in the city had a meeting this afternoon. We had to listen to the president of the Board of Education tell us that teaching is a business, and that we are all salesmen."

"That's swell, Miss Tibbs," Rudy said. "Can I go now?"

"No, because there's more. He said that our commodity as teachers is education and that all we have to do is sell it. And, now this is the important part. We must remember that we are no more than small cogs in a great educational machine."

"Oh," Rudy said. He was trying not to yawn.

"After the meeting," Miss Tibbs went on, "I met a teacher who refused to buy that particular line of hogwash. This man told me that he cares about each of his students and wants to see every single one be all that he or she can be. 'They don't always like what I require them to do,' he told me. 'But I'm not there to be a popular, Mr. Nice Guy salesman. I'm there to shape young lives.'"

"Sounds like a real swell fella, Miss Tibbs," Rudy said. "*Now* can I go?"

"His name was Stanley Keating."

Rudy stopped halfway out of his chair and stared at Miss Tibbs. Then he forced himself to grin. "You didn't fall for that applesauce, did you?" he said.

"There was nothing to fall for, Rudy. He was completely sincere. And no, you may not go, because I haven't gotten to the *most* important part yet." She leaned toward Rudy, her eyes serious. "I asked him if you were in one of his classes, and he said you were. He told me he was particularly concerned about you."

"Me?" Rudy said.

"Oh, yes. Imagine my surprise, Rudy, when he said that 'Mr. Hutchinson' was the class clown. That he refused to be serious about his work. That he looked for opportunities to take the easy way out. That he even went so far as to play pranks on other students right there in the classroom, and so cleverly he couldn't be caught." Miss Tibbs sat back in the chair and folded her arms across her apron top. "That sounded like the Rudy Hutchinson I had at the beginning of last year, not the Rudy Hutchinson I promoted from the sixth grade."

"Yeah, you're right," Rudy said. "He must have had me mixed up with somebody else."

"Mr. Keating has a marvelous command of the language. He described you to a T. What's going on, Rudy? Just at the time when your family needs for you to be the most grown-up, you decide to go backwards?"

"He's got it in for me! He picked me out the first day, and he hasn't let up on me since. And I haven't even done anything!"

"You had nothing to do with a certain cake-frosting incident?"

"He can't prove it."

"That isn't the point! The point is—"

Miss Tibbs paused, and her face clouded over as if suddenly she didn't know what the point was at all. Rudy was sure he couldn't tell her.

Why does she have to be around here all the time anyway? he thought. *She thinks she's Aunt Gussie now. She's not—and I don't have to listen to her!*

But he did hear her last words before she dismissed him from the kitchen. "Please don't let your father down," she said. "He's under enough pressure already."

He's not the only one, Rudy thought as he made his escape. But when he went upstairs to do some drawing, Dad's face kept appearing on the paper instead of Tarzan's or even Jesus'. It was a worried face, lined with Al Capone and Aunt Gussie and the stock market.

All right, he decided. *I'll just be so careful, nobody'll find out about any of my pranks. Especially not Dad.*

It was lively at the dinner table, with Dad there for a change, and Ingrid was too, as well as everybody else. There was enough noisy discussion to keep anyone from seeing Rudy loosen the top on the pepper shaker or noticing that he was slowly putting his spinach on Hildy Helen's plate or catching onto the fact that he was eating most of LaDonna's apple pie. It was the only thing edible on the table—and only because Ingrid had brought it from the bakery.

Dad, of course, didn't seem to notice *that* either. "Delicious dinner, ladies," he said.

"Hildy Helen and I finally discovered Betty Crocker," Miss Tibbs said. "Thank heaven for her cookbook."

"And for Bird's Eye frozen vegetables," Hildy Helen said. "That's what the spinach is." She looked at her plate. "And there's oodles of it. I didn't think the package was that big."

"That's good, Hildy," Rudy said. "We have to have our vitamins."

"I like a doll that eats her vitamins," Little Al said.

Hildy Helen took another large forkful.

When he'd done about everything he could get away with there, Rudy excused himself to take his plate into the kitchen, and then slipped soundlessly out the back door and re-entered through the front hall. They were still laughing and talking in the dining room, obviously unaware that he hadn't come back through, so he tiptoed on into the library and quietly opened Picasso's cage.

"Shh, Picasso," he whispered. "I got something for ya."

"Gustavia?" Picasso muttered. "Gustavia Nitz?"

"No, this is even better."

Rudy reached into his pocket and pulled out a balloon and a piece of string he'd gotten from a box of party decorations in the garage. He puffed the balloon full of air, tied it off with the string, and then looped the other end around Picasso's leg.

"Let's have some fun, birdie," Rudy said.

He set Picasso on the back of a chair and hurried from the library and out the side door. Seconds later he was back in the dining room, pouring the coffee.

"Thank you, Rudy," Dad said. "Don't mind if I do—"

He was cut off abruptly by a loud squawk from the library, followed by a crash.

"What's that bird up to?" Miss Tibbs said.

All eyes suddenly turned to Little Al, and Rudy felt a pang. He'd forgotten that Picasso was Little Al's responsibility. Anything that went wrong with that parrot—

But it was too late now. There was another loud crash, followed by a series of smaller ones, and Picasso let out a trail of screeches that went up Rudy's backbone. Everyone at the table rose as one and charged through the sitting room and across the hall.

But by the time they got to the library, there was no sign of Picasso except for the feathers he'd left strewn amid the ruins of two vases and a plaster bookend.

"Lord have mercy!" they heard someone else cry.

Once again there was a mad dash, this time for Aunt Gussie's room. Quintonia met them in the doorway, eyes on fire.

"I was down the hall in the washroom!" she said. "And I left Miss Gussie's door open so I could hear her. All of a sudden, that animal starts screaming, and she starts crying. And then I heard this loud pop, like a shot, and I thought somebody broke in the house and had gotten her with a—"

"No need to worry about that, Quintonia," Dad said. "I check the doors to make sure they're locked at all times, and if I don't, Rudy does."

Rudy wriggled past Quintonia and into Aunt Gussie's room before anyone could see the double guilt on his face.

Aunt Gussie was propped up in her bed, just as she had been several weeks before, the last time he'd been allowed to see her. The only difference now was that Picasso was perched on the pillow next to her, pecking at the string around his foot and muttering, "Gustavia. Miss Gustavia Nitz."

"I'll just put him back in his cage," Rudy said.

But Aunt Gussie shook her head, and the look she gave Rudy

stopped him before he even got close to the bed. She didn't make a sound. She didn't have to. Her one good eye clearly said, *I know this is your doing, Rudolph. I thought we talked about this.*

"Good night, Aunt Gussie," Rudy said. And he turned on his heel and hurried out of the room.

He also hurried past the group in the doorway. Everyone was staring at Little Al, and Dad was tapping his foot. Guilt gathering in his throat like Hildy Helen's pot roast, Rudy retreated to his room to read *God's Trombones.*

I'll apologize to Little Al when he comes up, he decided when he had read "The Prodigal Son" three times and still didn't know what it said. *And if Dad's given him a punishment, I'll tell Dad the truth, and I'll take it.*

But Al didn't come upstairs, even by the time LaDonna and Ingrid came down from LaDonna's room on the third floor and announced to Miss Tibbs that they were finished studying and they were going to have a snack before Ingrid left to catch a bus home.

"There's leftover pot roast," Miss Tibbs said.

"I think we'll have some apple pie, thanks," LaDonna told her.

Rudy was in the midst of mumbling, "I don't blame you," when he had an idea. The Picasso caper hadn't turned out exactly as he'd hoped, but he might still be able to scare Ingrid off from coming back here to torment him with her presence. Besides, it would just be fun.

As soon as he was sure the girls were in the kitchen—and he could even hear Hildy Helen in there with them, giggling shrilly the way she'd been doing lately—he crept out the front door and hid in the bushes just behind the bus stop. He could see the front door, but he knew Ingrid wouldn't be able to see him.

It seemed to take forever for them to eat their pie, and Rudy tried to concentrate on something else so his mouth wouldn't water. An early fall wind was kicking up, and he could hear the flag on top of Aunt Gussie's house flapping and the leaves on the oak in the front yard rustling against each other like crickets' legs. Summer was slowly fading into fall and taking with it the perfection of those last days in Cape Cod—his before-school outing with Aunt Gussie; his life before all she could do was moan and all people could do was tell him to grow up—not too much, but just enough.

He was grateful when the front door finally opened. Ingrid said one last good-bye to LaDonna before the door closed, and she skipped down the steps. The streetlight glowed like a halo on top of her blonde head as she crossed to the bus stop, but Rudy reminded himself that she was no angel.

Matter of fact, he thought, *I bet the devil sent her here just to make my life miserable.*

He held his breath as Ingrid leaned against the bus stop pole and surveyed the landscape. It seemed to Rudy that the girl never just relaxed. She was always on top of things, even when she was doing nothing.

But she wouldn't come out on top this time.

Rudy grinned to himself, sucked in a good breath, and let out a long, slow wail.

Ingrid didn't move.

She's scared stiff already, Rudy thought.

He wailed again, a little louder this time, and was just congratulating himself on how terrifying he sounded, when Ingrid suddenly turned around, snapped the bushes apart with her hands, and said, "Hutchinson, you really slaughter me, you know that?"

"Scared you, huh?" Rudy said.

"Oh, yeah, I'm quaking in my pumps here. Come out of there, you little urchin."

Rudy tried to keep grinning as he hauled himself from the bushes and brushed off a few stray leaves. It was hard, though. Ingrid seemed to be looking right through to the inside of his head.

"I was so right about you, Hutchinson," she said.

"You mean that I'm a swell fella?"

"No, that you're an immature boy who doesn't know when to quit playing around and grow up."

Rudy felt the top jiggling off his pressure keg. "At least I'm not a flat tire!" he said. "At least I try to get some fun out of life instead of taking everything so serious all the time."

"You haven't even seen serious yet. But you'll see it tomorrow. If it were up to me, I'd just fire you flat out. Since it's not, I just intend to work you so hard you'll finally quit." The bus appeared around the corner and Ingrid moved toward the curb. "Be ready, Hutchinson," she said.

Rudy watched the bus disappear before he started for the house, face toward the ground. He was so lost in thought, he didn't see the shadowy figure emerge from beside the steps until it was on him, and then he shouted so loud, they both jumped.

"It's me, Rudolpho," Little Al said. "Don't lose your supper or nothin'."

Rudy smeared his face with his hand in hopes of wiping off the panic. Little Al was watching him closely in the glare of the porch light.

"She didn't fall for it, huh?" he said.

"You saw?"

"Yeah."

Rudy shrugged. "I messed everything up tonight. I'm sorry about Picasso."

"Yeah, they all thought I done it. I told 'em I was sick of chasin' after that bird so I tried to tie him to his cage. Mr. Hutchie, he told me never to do it again—" Al glared at Rudy. "Which I *won't*."

"You want me to 'fess up?" Rudy said.

Little Al shook his head. "You don't hafta. I figure with whatever's eatin' you, you just need to find some better pranks to play is all."

"And how!"

"Since you seem to have a taste for that kinda thing again, I got a suggestion for ya."

Rudy nodded eagerly.

"This one's foolproof."

"You mean even I can't mess it up."

Little Al gave his crooked grin. "Yeah. Somethin' like that. Come on, I'll show ya."

They ran across the lawn and down the sidewalk toward 35th Street, avoiding the pools of light cast by the street lamps. Little Al stopped beside a pole which had a green box attached to it.

"You know about police call boxes, right, Rudolpho?"

"I know there's a phone locked in there. The cops use it to call into the station when they're out here prowling."

"And fellas like us use it to have some fun."

"You mean like make a prank call?" Rudy said.

"Sure. You know how many cops Capone's got on the take? Those saps deserve to have somebody givin' 'em the business, is what I say."

"But how are you gonna get to the phone?"

Little Al blinked at him. "Did you ever know a lock I couldn't pick, Rudolpho?"

"I guess not," Rudy said.

"Leave that to me."

Little Al fished in his pocket and pulled out a small piece of wire.

"Is that a hair pin?" Rudy said.

"I found it on the floor in the house, and I kept it. Ya never know when somethin' like this could come in handy, ya know what I mean?"

Rudy grinned. "I do now."

"You keep watch, and I'll open."

Rudy moved toward the curb, still careful to stay out of the light, and looked up and down the deserted street. It was too late for much traffic and too early for the street cleaner. Their timing was perfect.

"Ya know we gotta take advantage of these gadgets while we can," Little Al said as he worked at the lock. "I hear tell they started puttin' radios right in the police cars now so they don't even hafta get out to make a call."

"No kidding?" Rudy said.

"Nope. Got it!"

Rudy turned around to see Little Al grinning broadly and holding a phone receiver out to him.

"What do I do?" Rudy said.

"Just start talkin' when somebody answers," Little Al said. "Say somethin' like—"

But Rudy waved for him to be quiet as the phone clicked on the other end.

"Detective Bureau," a crisp, matter-of-fact voice said.

Rudy slammed the receiver down and looked wildly at Little Al.

"Whatsa matter? Why didn't ya say nothin'?"

"It was Detective Zorn," Rudy said. "You know what? I don't think I feel like doing this tonight." And without waiting for Al, he headed for the house.

Chapter Nine

*T*he first thing Rudy thought about when he woke up the next morning was not Detective Zorn or Ingrid or even Aunt Gussie and Picasso. The minute his eyes opened, he remembered that he had $1.50 in the pocket of his knickers to pay Van his club dues.

Then all I have to do is earn $3.50 more for the subscription and the supplies, he thought as he tore out from under the covers and searched for his knickers on the floor. *And I got plenty of supplies here. Maybe he'll just let me use these. Maybe I won't have to work for Ingrid that much longer after all.*

But his thoughts screeched to a halt when he stuck his hand into his knickers pocket and there was nothing there. Frantically he searched the other one, turned the pants upside down and shook them and crawled around on the floor and under the bed. But there was no money anywhere.

Rudy sat there, empty knickers in hand. *Where could I have lost it? I would have heard it fall out here in the house. I know I had it when I first got home.*

He was headed for the bedroom door before the thought was

89

even complete. Of course—it was out in the bushes where he'd hidden to scare Ingrid.

Barefoot and still in his plaid pajamas, Rudy slipped out the front door and ran across the lawn, the early autumn chill biting at his toes. He noticed nothing, however, but the ground under him as he scoured it with his eyes.

There was no $1.50 in the grass, nor on the sidewalk, nor in the middle of Prairie. Praying under his breath, he ran for the bushes, but he saw it before he even got there.

Hanging over the curbing like a piece of wet, wilted lettuce was a lone dollar bill, soaked just a few hours before by the street cleaner. When Rudy picked it up, it fell to pieces in his hand. The two quarters had probably floated south and were long gone down the storm drain.

After that, the day got worse and worse by the hour. Maury hid his gym shorts. Mr. Keating called on him six times during the grammar lesson. Hildy Helen went and sat with a bunch of girls and giggled all through lunch. And, worst of all, in activities period, Van announced that all membership money had to be in by next week when the contest started for which stories and illustrations were going to be in the fall edition of their magazine.

"How are your 'prospects' coming along, kid?" Van said to Rudy after the meeting.

"Uh, not bad," Rudy said. "I'll have the dues at least by next week, don't worry. And can I use my own supplies?"

Van flipped his hair around a couple of times and finally said, "Sure. And forget the subscription, too. No reason why you can't borrow my copy. You come up with a $1.50, and we'll call it square."

That made things look brighter for a few minutes, until Rudy realized it would take him two more weeks to earn that much, and he only had one.

"I'm never gonna make it," he told Hildy Helen and Little Al on the bus on the way home that afternoon. "I might as well quit my job right now and forget it. Maybe they got room for me in the Chumps' Club."

"You don't belong in no Chumps' Club, Rudolpho," Al said. His voice sounded a little fierce.

Hildy Helen, on the other hand, didn't say anything at all.

Rudy felt a bit lonely.

To make matters worse, Ingrid was as good as her word. That day, and for the rest of the week, she had a delivery list so long each afternoon, Rudy was sure she was paying people to call in orders just so he would have to pedal like a madman to get finished by five o'clock. Even on the two days it rained and the city was nothing but a sea of dripping umbrellas, people wanted freshly baked ginger snaps to go with their hot cocoa.

Dad says there's three million people in Chicago, he thought that Friday afternoon as he biked, soaked to the skin, back to Randolph Street. *And I think I've taken doughnuts to every one of them this week.*

The pavement was wet like a shadowed mirror, and the rain formed rings around the light from the street lamps. It was all very dark and eerie, and Rudy wanted to curl up with a cup of cocoa himself. But he knew all he had waiting for him at the bakery was Ingrid, ready to snarl at him because he'd dropped that cupcake in a puddle in the middle of a traffic jam on North Michigan Avenue. The lady who ordered them said it was all right that there were only 11 instead of a dozen, but Rudy was sure she'd called in just the same. In fact, he was sure that Ingrid was going to have it docked from his pay—and that the Argosy Club was just a dream that was never really going to come true no matter what.

But when he let himself in the back door of the bakery and shook the rain out of his clothes over the mat, it wasn't Ingrid who greeted him but Sylvia. Her smile was the most pleasant thing Rudy had seen in about a week.

"Oscar and Ingrid had a big party to cater tonight," she said. "Oscar said since you worked so hard this week, to pay you now." She reached for Rudy's hand and tucked a dollar bill into it.

"But it should only be 75 cents!" Rudy said.

Sylvia kept smiling as she said, "You're a good boy."

Rudy could barely say thank you for the lump in his throat. He wanted to get out of there fast before she could see that he was about to cry.

But Sylvia didn't take her hand away. She wrapped her fingers around Rudy's wrist and led him toward the front room.

"How about we have another frosting lesson, eh?" she said.

For a minute Rudy didn't know what she was talking about. Then when he remembered, the guilt was so huge, he couldn't do anything but take the cone from her and listen as she described how to make an icing rose.

So there he stood in the window of the Randolph Street Bakery that rainy Friday afternoon, practicing bright red roses on dainty cupcakes for all the world to see. It wouldn't have been so bad, really. Sylvia had talked herself out and was humming softly. The rain was muttering in a sort of friendly way out on the sidewalk. It was warm and dry and sweet-smelling in the bakery.

No, it really wouldn't have been so bad—if that world outside looking in hadn't included Maury Worthington.

Rudy was perfecting his best effort yet when he heard an unmistakably familiar hoot from the other side of the front window. He looked right up into Maury's pimpled face. It was pressed so close, Rudy could see the stubby black hairs on his upper lip.

"Oh no!" Rudy said before he could stop himself.

Sylvia looked up and broadened her smile and waved for Maury and the man beside him to come in. Rudy had only seen Maury's father once before and then only for a few seconds, but he was sure the even-bigger-than-Maury man was Mr. Worthington. He shook his head and gave Maury a sharp nudge. Mercifully, they moved on down the sidewalk with their umbrellas, but not before Maury gave one more loud, nasty hoot that set Rudy's cheeks blazing.

That'll be all over Hirsch by Monday, he thought miserably. It was all he could do not to run after him with a cone full of red frosting.

I'll get back at him, Rudy decided. *I just have to be careful not to get caught.*

With a dollar in his pocket and something to plan, Rudy's spirits lifted, even as he rode home in the rain with the newspaper Sylvia gave him propped over his head. He almost couldn't wait to get Little Al and Hildy together to help him come up with the perfect scheme.

But Al wasn't home when he got there, and Miss Tibbs said he had left a note saying he wouldn't be there for supper; he had something important to do. When he went looking for Hildy Helen, she was in her room, sprawled across her bed with her eyes closed.

"You're taking a *nap*?" Rudy said.

But she didn't answer.

The only person who was available for co-scheming was LaDonna. But when she stormed into Rudy's room, he knew right away this wasn't the time to try to get *her* help.

"Sol again?" Rudy said.

LaDonna tore off her rain cape and flung it over Rudy's bedpost. "This has been the worst day of my life," she said.

Rudy saw that the matching suit underneath was covered in little droplets of mud that looked like brown confetti against the yellow serge. LaDonna was particular about her clothes, but he'd never seen her get this mad over a little rain damage before.

The brown gloves came off as she ticked items on her fingers. "First, two other witnesses backed out of the Eliot Ness investigation because they're frightened by the threats they've received. Second, I had to ride the bus because it's obvious Sol has some kind of mental block against picking me up—ever—in my entire life. And that was all right, because Mr. Jim paid me today so I had the bus fare, but then some hoodlum stole my handbag! Snatched it and ran off with it, just like that!"

She snapped her fingers and then flopped down onto Little Al's bed. "I simply can't win, no matter what I do!"

Rudy swallowed hard. "That wouldn't have happened if you'd been riding with Sol."

"No kidding, Rudy. How *ever* did you figure that out?"

Rudy wanted to crawl under the bed. But he pasted on a grin and said, "They teach us that stuff in seventh grade."

"Well, I wish they'd teach you how to organize this impossible man! I think I'm going to ask Ingrid to give it a try."

"Ingrid!" Rudy said. "We don't need her!"

"Evidently we do. She can give you a set of instructions a lot more complicated than the ones you give Sol, and you never make a mistake on a delivery."

"Yeah, but I'm not deaf. Of course, Ingrid writes it all down for me—"

Rudy stopped in mid-sentence, and LaDonna sat up slowly on the bed. They looked at each other for a full 15 seconds.

"Well, whatta you know," LaDonna said. "An idea."

She marched over to Rudy's desk, picked up a pencil and a piece of paper, and brought them to him.

"If I were you, I wouldn't come out of this room until I had written out a schedule for Sol for Monday."

She started for the door, but Rudy said, "Wait a minute. Here."

LaDonna looked down at the dollar bill Rudy had fished from his pocket and was holding out to her.

"What's that for?" she said.

"To help replace some of the money that was in your purse."

"You don't have to do that."

"Yes, I do."

LaDonna searched his face for a minute, and then she reached down for the dollar. Her fingers pressed slightly against Rudy's palm.

"Thank you," she said.

When she was gone, Rudy started on the schedule. Miss Tibbs brought him a peanut butter and jelly sandwich, since, she said, no one seemed to want dinner. When he had finished it and the schedule, Little Al still wasn't home, so Rudy got out his drawing things and sat in the window to watch for him. All he could do, though, was chew on his pencil and then finally draw a picture of Jesus surrounded by a cloud of confusion.

Maybe I'm not getting any answers to any of these prayers because I'm not handling my responsibilities very well, he thought. Why should Jesus clear this up when I could probably do it myself if I quit messing everything up?

He tossed the drawing in the trash and went back to chewing the pencil.

Maybe Little Al's going back to some of his old ways, just like I am, Rudy thought. *He misses Aunt Gussie, too.*

But that train of thought derailed and wrecked his head. Little Al's "old ways" could land the boy in jail.

Little Al didn't end up behind bars *that* night, anyway. He came in around eight o'clock, yawning and stretching and heading straight for his bed.

"Hey, no ya don't!" Rudy said. "Where've you been?"

"Out," Little Al said. "Can we talk about this in the morning, Rudolpho? I hate to beef, but I'm beat. My dogs are tired. My gams feel like they're made a lead."

And before he could get the next "beef" out he was sound asleep.

It was suddenly far too quiet in the room. Even the rain had stopped its muttering outside, and all Rudy could hear were his own thoughts. Determined to wake Hildy Helen up this time, he went down the hall to her room and turned the doorknob.

But the door was locked. Hildy Helen never locked her door, and Rudy felt his heart already starting to sink as he knocked and waited for an explanation.

But there was none—only the sound of Hildy Helen's muffled sobbing.

Chapter Ten

*T*hat weekend was probably the longest in Rudy Hutchinson's life.

Little Al disappeared all day Saturday, telling Rudy he had "a little business to take care of."

LaDonna was holed up Saturday night and most of Sunday on the third floor with Ingrid, studying for college entrance exams. The only time they took off was to go to Ingrid's church together.

Even though Little Al and Hildy Helen went to Sunday school with Rudy as always, Al kept dozing off, and Hildy Helen was as distant as if she'd been back in Shelbyville. Rudy tried everything from drawing a picture of Little Al snoozing during the sermon to singing the hymns like an opera star to get her to smile. Nothing worked.

Sunday afternoon, Hildy got on the phone with her friend Agnes Anne and giggled and after that acted as if everything was just fine, but she still wouldn't let Rudy in on why she'd been crying herself to sleep on Friday night.

"You must have been dreaming, Rudy," she said. "I slept like a baby."

Dad, of course, was occupied with the Eliot Ness investigation, and Miss Tibbs sat in the library all weekend correcting papers, so Rudy couldn't even listen to the radio.

Why doesn't she just move in here? Rudy thought irritably. *She's here all the time anyway.*

He was almost thankful when Monday morning came so he could get out of there. That is, until Maury shouted across the gymnasium as they lined up for inspection, "Hey, Hutchinson! Did you bring any of your frosting roses with you today?"

"Frosting roses?" said one of the other fellas.

"Yeah. Didn't you know that Hutchinson decorates cakes down at the bakery on Randolph Street?"

"Are you just razzin' us?" somebody else said.

"Yeah, he is," Rudy said. "You can't believe a word he says."

"You callin' me a liar, Hutchinson?" Maury said. "I stood right there at the window and watched ya!" He turned to the other boys who by now had gathered into an interested knot. "He had his frosting in a little cone, and with his pinkie stuck out like this—"

And then suddenly Maury stopped. "Hey," he said, eyes squinting in his pudgy face, "you can't say you didn't pull that frosting trick on my sister, 'cause I got the goods on you now. What if I go to Keating, huh?"

"What if you do?" Rudy said. "I know Mr. Keating. He's gonna say, 'Mr. Worthington, come back when you can speak to me in proper grammar.' Which means you'll never come back, because you never will. Right, Maury?"

The coach's whistle blew just then, and Rudy went smiling to his position in line. But inside, the pressure was building again. He had to do something, or he was going to come open. He was sure he couldn't juggle all the responsibility that was being heaped on him. If he didn't do something downright irresponsible, he was going to blow a gasket.

Just before Coach dismissed the class to hit the showers, Rudy slipped into the locker room and tied Maury's oxford bags into a knot. The pressure let off, just a little.

So in English the next day, he grabbed Dorothea's composition book while she was away from her desk sharpening her pencil and slipped in the poem he'd typed on Aunt Gussie's typewriter the night before. When the teacher asked who wanted to read aloud his or her original poem which he'd assigned for homework, Dorothea's hand was the first to shoot up.

But one glance at her notebook, and her already colorless face grew even more pale.

"What is it, Miss Worthington?" Mr. Keating said.

"I'd rather not read mine, sir," she said.

"But you had your hand up. There's something on your paper. It's even typed. You always go the extra mile, don't you, Miss Worthington? Go ahead. Read it."

"No, really—this isn't—"

"For crying out loud!" Mr. Keating said.

Teaching was obviously becoming more frustrating than he'd expected. He snatched up the poem and at once began to read:

"C-U-T-E
Don't you wish you looked like me?
D-I-V-I-N-E
Bet you want some hair like mine
P-R-E-T-T-Y
When boys see me they pass you by
Bing-bang-bash-boom
I'm the prettiest girl in this whole room—"

"Mr. Keating, please stop!" Dorothea cried. "I didn't write that!"

Mr. Keating looked at her blankly. "Then who did?"

Dorothea couldn't speak. She just turned around and stabbed a bony finger toward Rudy. Mr. Keating shook his head.

"I don't think you can blame this one on Mr. Hutchinson. He's too lazy to take the trouble to *type* something just for a joke. Besides—I don't think he's capable of something quite this clever.

Are you, Mr. Hutchinson?"

Rudy grinned. "No, sir, Mr. Keating. As usual, you're right."

The pressure let off some more—until activities period, when Rudy had to make still another excuse for not having his dues.

So that afternoon, he gathered up all the sawdust he could find in woodworking class and stuffed it inside Maury's hat, which was hanging on a peg by the door. He left the minute the bell rang, but he could hear Maury yelling from all the way down the hall.

The pressure was off again. Rudy felt a bit guilty about embarrassing Dorothea and Maury. But he consoled himself with the thought that they'd done plenty of mean things to him, so he was just getting even.

After several days of stealing all the chalk from Mr. Keating's room, hiding Coach's whistle, and doing oodles of other tricks that were driving half of Hirsch Junior High School crazy, Rudy convinced himself that it was helping him survive.

It was the only way, he told himself as he tried to balance two German chocolate cakes on his handlebars, that he could get through Ingrid's torrent of criticism every day.

"Why did it take you two hours to make 10 deliveries, Hutchinson?" she would say. Or, "Not bad, but wait until you see what I have for you tomorrow. You'll never pull that off."

He always did, but he told himself it was only because he was switching sandwiches in lunch boxes and sticking library books back in the wrong places.

The one person he never tried to prank was Ingrid herself, but she imagined his trickery in everything he did.

"Do I dare open this?" she would say when he returned at the end of the day with his empty box. "Or is something going to fly out at me?"

"Does Mrs. Robertson really want a hundred more petits fours for her party," she asked when he came in with a new order, "or are you making that up?"

Sylvia smiled and Oscar chuckled through it all. But the day Rudy was so tired he dropped a coconut custard pie before he even got out the door, he wasn't sure how they felt.

"You did that on purpose, didn't you, Hutchinson?" Ingrid said. "I'm surprised you didn't 'accidentally' drop it in my face."

"Leave him alone," Oscar said. "Just clean it up, Rudy."

But Rudy was certain he saw doubt in the baker's eyes. Even when Sylvia patted his arm and said, "He's a good boy," Rudy didn't think her smile was quite as sincere as usual.

On the way home that day, he couldn't even think of a trick to play to make himself feel better.

The one good thing that happened as the days went by was that Sol was managing to pick up and deliver everyone in the Hutchinson family on time and in the proper places by using Rudy's written schedule. That definitely put LaDonna in a better frame of mind each evening when she came home from work. Even though she brought Ingrid with her half the time, Rudy was at least grateful that there were no more ranting scenes in his room.

She did come in one night before supper and perch on the edge of Little Al's empty bed. He, of course, wasn't home yet, as usual.

"What's eating you, Rudy?" she said.

"Me?"

"You're the only Rudy in this room. You haven't been yourself lately. How can I help?"

"I'm doing all right," Rudy said.

It was funny. He'd been longing for someone to talk to, but now that someone was offering to listen, he felt like a chump trying to put it into words. How was it going to sound to her if he said, *Ingrid's picking on me* or *I'm afraid of Maury Worthington* or *LaDonna, I just don't want to grow up—it's too hard!* And talking about Aunt Gussie was completely out of the question.

There was only one subject that would even come out of his

mouth, and Rudy hurried to bring it up before LaDonna could do any more prying.

"I'll tell you who's got something eating them, and that's Hildy Helen."

"Roller-coaster moods?" LaDonna said.

"Huh?"

"One minute she's giggling like a fool and the next she's crying so hard she can barely breathe?"

"Yeah!"

"She's 12-going-on-13, Rudy. It's in her contract."

"What contract?"

"Forget it. It's just girls that age. I was emotional like that myself when I was 12."

"Why?"

"You don't know what it's like to be female," LaDonna said. "You're expected to be perfect, and of course you can't be, so sometimes all you can do is cry."

"I don't care if she's perfect," Rudy said. "I just want her to talk to me like she always did!"

He hadn't meant for that to come out. LaDonna was nodding sagely. "I see," she said.

"No, you don't. I don't even see," Rudy said.

"Let me see what I can do," LaDonna said.

"Like what?"

"Leave it to me. You and Al just be boys for a couple of days, and I'll find out what I can." She looked around. "Where is he, anyway?"

That was another thing. Rudy willed his shoulders not to sag. He sure didn't want her to see him mooning over Little Al. And besides, what if Al was out there getting himself into trouble? Now that LaDonna was working for Dad, she'd have to tell him.

Of course, the mature thing to do would be to tell Dad in the first place.

But how mature was he supposed to be?

It was all he could do not to scream.

LaDonna worked fast. That very evening she gained entrance into Hildy Helen's room, with Ingrid in tow. In five minutes, they were all giggling, Hildy Helen loudest and most shrilly of all.

Oh, so now she'll talk to LaDonna and Ingrid, but not to me, Rudy thought.

When he heard them all troop downstairs, still whispering and cackling like hens, he shoved aside his drawing and his homework and concentrated on his next prank. Maybe he'd play it on Hildy Helen herself, just to get her attention.

Suddenly, the giggles downstairs turned to shrieks, and Rudy rolled his eyes. Why couldn't they just laugh? Why did they have to scream as if somebody was being scalped?

But the howling grew louder, and it was only another minute before Rudy realized they weren't having a good time. They were genuinely afraid of something.

Rudy flung himself off his bed and raced downstairs. LaDonna, Hildy Helen, and Ingrid were all standing in the front hall, staring into an open box. Even Ingrid was white-faced.

"What's wrong?" Rudy said.

"As if you didn't know!" LaDonna cried. She held the box out in front of her with a shaky hand.

"I *don't* know!" Rudy said. "What's in there?"

For answer, Ingrid began spewing out German, Hildy Helen clapped her hands over her mouth, and LaDonna put her hand on her hip—a sure sign that Rudy was about to get a lecture.

"This was not a bit funny, Rudolph Hutchinson! In fact, it's downright grisly. I hope our screaming didn't upset Aunt Gussie. She's liable to have another stroke. I nearly had one myself!"

Rudy could stand it no longer. He stepped forward and snatched the box out of her hand. But when he looked in it, he wished he hadn't.

Inside the box was a large, wet, dead rat. Its front legs were tied together, and so were its back ones, and there was a plug of cotton that reeked of gas in its mouth. Rudy felt the supper in his stomach threatening to make a reappearance.

"Don't think you're going to convince us that you didn't put this inside the front door," LaDonna said. "Because none of us is going to believe it. It has you written all over it."

"Tell them, Hildy Helen!" Rudy said. "I'd never do something this bad!"

Hildy opened her mouth, but then she looked from Ingrid to LaDonna and shut it again.

"You know I wouldn't!" Rudy said.

Hildy Helen only shrugged.

"All right, if you didn't, who did?" Ingrid said, this time in English. "The doors are all locked, right? It was *inside* when we found it."

It was Rudy's turn to open his mouth and then shut it. If the door had been locked, it wasn't because he'd locked it. Although he'd promised Dad he'd see to it that they were all safely secured inside when he wasn't there, Rudy had been so busy with thoughts of Hildy Helen, he'd forgotten.

So do I tell them I left the door unlocked and let them go into hysterics again? Or do I just let them think I did it and let them yell at me?

Rudy cleared his throat. "I guess I got a little carried away this time," he said.

"I guess you did," LaDonna said. "Get this disgusting thing out of here before Miss Tibbs gets back from her P.T.A. meeting."

"Lucky for you Quintonia's giving Aunt Gussie her bath," Hildy Helen said. "I don't think they can hear from the washroom with the water running."

"Go bury it in the backyard," Ingrid said. "And then go take a bath yourself. Uck!"

Anybody else want to tell me what to do? Rudy thought as he carried the box out through the hall door to the courtyard. And all because he was trying to keep them from getting more scared.

I guess I deserve it, Rudy thought as he found a garden shovel by the stone shed and started to dig.

But as he picked up the box to lower it into the hole he'd made, something struck him.

He was the only one who knew he hadn't done it—except for the person who *did* do it.

It had to be Maury Worthington, Rudy thought quickly. *Who else? I never did anything this bad to him or his high-hat sister. But, then, if this was Maury—*

Or was it? Rudy took a deep breath and took another look inside the box at the dead rat. With its limbs all tied up and that gag in its mouth, it was pretty gruesome, even for Maury. The doubt was enough to make Rudy shake the box and stir up a piece of paper from beneath the lifeless little body.

Being careful not to touch it, Rudy dumped the rat into the hole and with the tips of two fingers pulled out the piece of paper. The moment he read it, he let it fall from his grasp as if it were on fire.

You're a rat, Jim Hutchinson, the note said. *This is what happens to rats. Mark it.*

✢ ⬧ ✢

Chapter Eleven

*M*ark it.

Rudy stood frozen and tried to remember what that meant. He'd heard Little Al say it before. Was it about—

Then he snapped from his freeze, and his heart began to pound again. Maybe it didn't matter. Maybe what mattered was that it was Mob language. This wasn't just something he could bury to keep himself out of trouble.

Rudy *did* bury the rat in a shallow grave, but he tucked the note into his pocket before he headed into the house. He found Ingrid and LaDonna standing by the front door, book bags in hand.

"You're going out?" Rudy said. By now his heart was pounding in his ears.

"We're going to Ingrid's up in Portage Park to study," LaDonna said.

"Who can concentrate around here?" Ingrid said. "No offense, LaDonna."

"None taken."

They started for the door, and Rudy's mouth burst open.

"No!" he said. "Don't go!"

"What is this, Hutchinson—a ploy to stall us while you get some other lovely little trick going? Nothing doing!"

"No, I just wanted to say—"

"You wanted to say you were sorry?" LaDonna said, smiling too sweetly. "Isn't that nice. But it's too late, all right? Now just run along, and try not to get into any more trouble until Miss Tibbs and your father get home."

"Dad!" Rudy cried.

"That's his name," Ingrid said dryly.

"Where is he?"

"He's—"

"Don't tell him, LaDonna!" Ingrid said. "You're setting the poor man up!"

"I want to know where he is!"

Rudy was so close to crying, his throat was beginning to close. LaDonna looked at him closely.

"What's going on, Rudy?" she said.

"I just want to talk to him. I'm all mixed up!"

"That's the first thing you've ever said that I actually believe," Ingrid said.

LaDonna sighed. "He's at his office, finishing up his report for Mr. Ness. But he'll be home soon. You can talk to him then."

Rudy managed to stifle a final cry and nodded. "I'll lock the door behind you," he said.

Ingrid grunted. "Yeah, since we have people leaving little packages."

The minute they were gone, Rudy ran to the library window and watched them until they boarded the bus.

I should have warned them, he thought. *But then what if nothing happened? They'd just say I was being a prankster. Why did I ever start that again?*

But there was no time to think about that now. He grabbed the phone and asked the operator to connect him to Dad's office.

"I'm sorry," she said after a pause that lasted a lifetime. "That line is busy."

I have to go there, Rudy told himself. *I have to at least tell Dad—even if it does turn out to be a false alarm.*

But how could it be? The question got his heart pounding so loud in his ears that he didn't hear Hildy Helen come into the room, and when he turned to leave the library, he let out a shout at the sight of her in the doorway.

She'd been crying again.

"Sometimes I hate everything, Rudy," she said tearfully. "Don't you?"

Rudy clenched his hands at his sides. *Now* she wanted to talk. Why did everything have to be so complicated?

"Yeah, sometimes I do," he said. "But could we talk—"

"Those girls are so hateful! They came in my room and made me feel like I was one of them—and then they went off and left me! I begged LaDonna to let me go with them, but she wouldn't!"

"Oh," Rudy said.

"I thought they understood, too, when I told them all my problems."

"Uh-huh." Rudy edged closer to the door. Hildy Helen didn't seem to notice.

"Don't you ever just wish you had somebody to talk to that *knows*? I miss Aunt Gussie so much!"

"Yeah, me too," Rudy said. He took another step into the doorway. "You can talk to me anytime, except—"

"Except I can't, Rudy, not about this. See, it's about boys."

Rudy didn't even answer this time. He just moved out the library door. Hildy Helen moved with him.

"I know *you're* a boy. That's not what I mean," she said. "It's *other* boys. I'm such a dumb Dora around them. They think I'm just a pig's coattail, and they're probably right. I want to be a bearcat—you know, someone who can stand her own like Ingrid—

or a baby vamp—someone boys notice, like LaDonna."

Even if he hadn't been so anxious to get to his father that he was chewing a hole in his lip, Rudy was sure he wouldn't have known what in the world she was talking about.

"Look, Hildy Helen," he said, "I think you're already baby bear and all that stuff, but right now—"

"I *knew* you wouldn't understand!" Hildy Helen cried. And with that she was gone, across the hall and up the stairs. Rudy heard her door slam before he could even move.

For once he was glad for roller-coaster moods.

Rudy listened for Quintonia, but she was obviously still helping Aunt Gussie with her bath. Rudy buttoned his sweater and headed for the front door. When the doorbell rang, he jumped a foot.

His first impulse was to dash out the back door, but even as he ran toward the sitting room, he knew that was a bad idea. If it was the Mob, they'd have men all over the property. And besides, when did the Mob ever come to the front door? What if it was Dad, and he'd forgotten his key? Dad was absent-minded like that sometimes.

The doorbell rang again, impatiently, and Rudy rubbed the sweat from his palms onto the sides of his knickers and went for it. Very slowly he turned the knob and opened it a crack.

There in the glare of the porch light stood Maury Worthington's father.

It was the shock of it that moved Rudy to open the door all the way. Mr. Worthington didn't wait for an invitation but shoved past Rudy and into the front hall. He already had his hat off and was peering into the library by the time Rudy got the door closed.

"Where is your father?" he said. "I want to speak to him."

"He isn't here," Rudy said. *And I wish he were, believe me, for more reasons than one!* He also wished Picasso were here in the library instead of in Aunt Gussie's room. He could always be counted on to say something rude at times like this.

"Where is the old lady then?" Mr. Worthington said. "Where's your aunt? Isn't she responsible for you, too?"

If Rudy had hackles, he knew they'd be standing up at this point. "Aunt Gussie isn't an old lady," he said between his teeth. "And she's too sick to come out."

"Sorry to hear that," Mr. Worthington said, just the way he probably would have said "excuse me" to somebody on the El train. "Who is looking after you kids?"

"Nobody," Rudy said.

"That figures." Mr. Worthington took one more searing look around the front hall to satisfy himself that Rudy wasn't hiding any legal guardians in Aunt Gussie's artifacts, and then he bore down on Rudy. His face was suddenly a bigger, meaner version of Maury's—and it scared Rudy more than Maury's ever had.

"Now you listen here," he said. "My boy has told me what's going on at that school with you laying traps in his path everywhere he goes. Do you deny it?"

Rudy didn't have a chance to. Mr. Worthington plunged on.

"I didn't believe him at first, especially after I saw you making roses in the bakery. But when my daughter chimed in, I knew it was true. My Dorothea couldn't tell a lie if her life depended on it. So you listen here—"

As if Rudy had a choice. Mr. Worthington's voice had risen to a roar, and his face was turning purple, just the way Maury's did when he was ranting.

"—if you don't lay off my kids, there's going to be real trouble. *Real* trouble!"

The color of Mr. Worthington's face was beginning to concern Rudy. If the man didn't calm down, Rudy was sure he was going to explode. He knew how that felt.

"Sure, Mr. Worthington," Rudy said.

"I got enough problems without having to worry about them," he went on, as if Rudy hadn't even spoken. "A man thinks he's making a fortune for his family, and what happens? The stock market goes nuts—and then I go nuts! Before I know it, I can't sleep, I can't eat. I'm screaming like a banshee!"

Rudy believed that. He was doing it now, and his entire tweed overcoat was quivering as if the man in it were about to fly apart.

"All right, Mr. Worthington," Rudy said. "I'll lay off your kids."

"What?" Mr. Worthington's head snapped back to Rudy. "What did you say?"

"I said all right. I'll lay off your kids."

For a moment the man stared at Rudy as if he'd just spoken in Greek. Then slowly the purple in his face faded, and he gave a sharp nod.

"See that you do or, like I said, there's going to be trouble."

"Trouble?" said someone from the hallway. "Is there trouble out here, Mr. Rudy?"

Rudy's heart leapt as he looked at Quintonia, hurrying toward them, still drying her hands on a towel.

"No trouble," Mr. Worthington said. "We got it taken care of, the kid and me."

"Is that right, Mr. Rudy?"

"Yes!" Rudy said. He just wanted everyone to leave him alone so he could get to his father before somebody else did.

Mr. Worthington seemed as anxious to leave as he did and made a hasty departure out the front door. But Quintonia wasn't in quite such a hurry. She put her hand on Rudy's shoulder and said, "You sure you're all right?"

"Couldn't be better!" Rudy said.

"Is that what you want me to tell your aunt?"

"Aunt Gussie?"

Quintonia just lifted her eyebrows.

"She asked about me?" Rudy said.

"Of course she did. She heard all this ruckus out here when she got out of the bath, and she started moaning and pointing like she does every time she hears your voice, and nothing will do but I have to come out and find out if you're all right."

"She does that?"

"Why do I have to answer every question twice?" Quintonia said. "Yes, she does that just about every day."

Rudy bit his lip before he could ask another question. There wasn't time now anyway. But knowing Aunt Gussie was missing him just the way he was missing her slowed his heartbeat down and settled the confusion in his head just a little.

"Tell her I'm fine," he said. "Really. Me and Mr. Worthington, we just had a matter to discuss."

"Uh-huh," Quintonia said.

She gave Rudy a long look before she finally swished back to Aunt Gussie's room and closed the door behind her. This time Rudy didn't hesitate. The delay had given him time to come up with a good idea, but he wanted to get on it before somebody else could interrupt him.

Rudy dashed upstairs for the day's schedule for Sol and quickly filled in another assignment. Then he carried it with him out to the garage apartment where Sol was just putting his feet up for the night.

"Sorry, Sol," Rudy shouted at him. "We have another run to make."

He showed Sol the schedule and then handed him his shoes. "I'll go with you to keep you company!" Rudy shouted and practically shoved Sol's shoes onto his feet.

When they pulled up in the Pierce Arrow to the office on Dearborn Street, Rudy told Sol to wait in the car and he would go in and get Dad. He shouted it twice, just to make sure Sol didn't misunderstand and drive off without either one of them.

All was dark beyond the revolving door as Rudy pushed his way in, except for the dim light the cleaning lady was using to scrub the floor by.

She was on her hands and knees, squeezing a soapy rag into a scrub bucket, when Rudy skirted the wet spots to get to the elevator.

"You're out late," she said. She didn't look up as she spoke, but kept on scrubbing at the stains left by the lawyers and secretaries whose feet had been tromping in and out all day. "Who you think you're gonna see at this hour?"

"My father," Rudy said. He pushed the button on the elevator and watched the arrow above the door move up with maddening slowness.

"Who's your father?" she said.

For crying out loud! Rudy wanted to scream at her. *I don't have time to talk!*

He glanced down at her as once again she squeezed out her rag so carefully into the bucket. He could see that her fingernails were blue within her swollen fingertips. It sent a pang through him.

"My dad's James Hutchinson," Rudy said as politely as he could.

The cleaning lady's pasty face burst into a smile. "He's aces, that James Hutchinson! He's as decent to the cleaning crew as he is to them fancy pantses in the finance office."

Rudy nodded and stole another look at the elevator arrow. Just a few more floors to go.

"Your pop's here, all right," she went on. "He's got some men with him, too. They come in the back door just a little bit ago. They asked me where his office was, and I was happy to tell 'em. 'You're in for a treat,' I says to 'em. 'That Mr. Hutchinson, he's aces—'"

"Did you say they came in the *back* door?" Rudy said.

The cleaning lady stopped with her rag hanging over the bucket and gave that some thought. "Yessir, it was the back door. I remember it, seein' how I hadn't got that far yet and they didn't have to walk on my clean floor to get to the elevator—not that I woulda said nothin', mind you. I know my place, though your pop, Mr. Hutchinson—he's aces—he don't care nothin' about a person's place. He treats us all the same."

Rudy didn't hear the rest. The elevator opened, and he dove in and operated the controls himself.

Nobody comes in the back door! was all Rudy could think as the elevator made its too-slow climb to Dad's floor. *If somebody came in the back to see Dad, it's because they were sneaking. The men didn't want anybody to see them. Dad's in big trouble!*

Rudy was nearly sick by the time the elevator doors opened, and he crept against the wall toward Dad's office. When he got within view of the foggy window on the office door, his worst fear was realized.

There were two silhouettes against the glass, both wearing fedoras pulled over their faces, both standing still and squaring their padded shoulders the way the Mob always did. Rudy put his hand on his mouth to keep from throwing up.

Come on, you gotta do something! he told himself. *You can't let them get Dad!*

At first, Rudy's brain seemed to freeze. What did he know about fighting the Mob?

What do I know about anything *anymore except playing jokes? Why am I a chump? Jesus, please forgive me. Help me, please!*

On the other side of the foggy-glassed window, one of the men waved his hand, and Rudy gasped. He was holding something, and he'd seen enough of them to know. It had to be a gun.

I wish I were back at school playing a joke! he thought frantically. *I know how to do that! I'd just pick up something and—*

Suddenly, Rudy whirled around. There was a chair and a small table in the hall, and on it was a painted vase. Rudy grabbed it and went to the door.

Just pretend you're playing a prank, he told himself. *Just do it!*

And squeezing his eyes shut tight, he smashed the vase through the office window.

✠ ✠ ✠

Chapter Twelve

The glass seemed to hit the floor forever, each piece smashing, and then smashing again, and then shattering yet a third time. In the midst of it there was a torrent of shouting that hit Rudy and bounced off—all but one sentence that got him between the eyes and stayed there:

"Freeze! Put your hands up! We are law enforcement officers!"

Rudy opened his eyes slowly, and cringed at the sight before him.

There in the window was Dad—and Detective Zorn—and Eliot Ness. Detective Zorn lowered his gun. Mr. Ness returned his cigar to his mouth. Rudy prayed that the floor would open up and suck him through.

"Rudy, what on *earth*?"

"I'm sorry! I'm sorry—" Rudy stammered as he backed away.

The door came open, and Dad crunched his way through the broken glass. "What were you thinking?"

"I thought it was the Mob! The cleaning lady said they came in the back door, and you never let anybody come in the back door, so I thought they were trying to get in without anybody seeing them.

Honest! And then I thought I saw him with a gun, only it was his cigar—"

"We *were* trying to get in without somebody seeing us," Detective Zorn said. "The Mob!"

"Oh," Rudy said. His face felt as if he'd been attacked by bees. "I just thought—"

"That's the problem—you think too much!" Dad said. Rudy was sure he'd never seen his father that tight and angry before, even the time Rudy and Hildy Helen had dipped the Shelbyville sheriff's cigar in horse dung. And this time it hadn't been a prank at all.

"It was an honest mistake, Jim," Mr. Ness said in his quiet voice. "He was just trying to protect you."

Dad was pinching the bridge of his nose with his fingers. "I know, but what were you doing here in the first place, Rudy?"

"I wanted to give you this." Rudy dug into his pocket and produced the note. "It came in a box with a dead rat."

Dad looked at the paper, and his mouth flattened out. He handed it to Mr. Ness.

"How did you get here?" Dad said to Rudy.

"Sol. He's waiting downstairs."

"All right, you go get in the car and wait for me. I'll finish up here, and we'll talk about this at home."

Rudy didn't even look at Detective Zorn or Mr. Ness as he hurried, head down, to the elevator. He was glad the cleaning lady had moved on to another floor when he got to the lobby, because he was too teared up to talk.

Why can't I do anything right lately? he thought. *I am a chump. Jesus, are You not helping me because I've messed up so much? Is it because I went back to my old ways?*

That didn't sound like the Jesus he'd always drawn—the Jesus they talked about at the Second Presbyterian Church.

But maybe he'd had *that* wrong, too.

Dad didn't say much on the way home, and Rudy wasn't going to ask him any questions to get him started. Dad finally spoke just as Sol was driving up to the house. Rudy saw Al slipping in the front door.

"Where in the world has he been at this time of night?" Dad said.

"I don't know," Rudy said. "Honest—he won't tell me."

Rudy thought he saw a flicker of fear go through Dad's eyes, but it was gone as quickly as it came. Dad's face was soft by the time he got the two boys together in the library and a swollen-eyed Hildy Helen had been summoned down to join them.

"I know this is a hard time," Dad said to the three of them, "and I know I've given you a lot of responsibility. But I want you to have a normal life—to be like other kids."

But when I act like a kid, everybody hates that, too! Rudy wanted to shout.

Then for a minute he thought he *had* said it, because Dad was looking at him hard, with that flicker going through his eyes again, as if he were afraid.

"I hate the fact that you have to imagine the worst," Dad said. "I know I have put you in that position myself. But it's going to be all right. Please, please, try not to worry so much."

His voice broke off, and he put his forehead in his hand. "Go on to bed. We'll talk about this tomorrow."

"What happened, Rudy?" Hildy Helen whispered as they trooped upstairs.

Rudy told them, and they listened with their mouths open.

"He saw you coming in, too, Little Al," he said as he finished.

Little Al let out a long, slow whistle. "I think we're gonna be in big trouble once Mr. Hutchie gets this worked out in his head, Rudolpho."

"I don't care," Hildy Helen said. "My life is so awful anyway. I just don't care!"

She flounced off to her room, and Rudy and Little Al looked blankly at each other.

"At least we got one thing goin' for us, Rudolpho," Little Al said. "We ain't girls."

Dad had already left for work the next morning when they got up, which meant a whole day in school with visions of their punishments haunting their heads. And that wasn't the worst of it. Maury was waiting for Rudy when he got to the gymnasium.

"Hey, Hutchinson," he said as he stood up from tying his shoes. "I hear you had a visitor last night."

It took Rudy a second to remember Mr. Worthington. Too much had happened since then.

"Oh, yeah," he said.

He headed for his place in line, but Maury blocked his way with his bulky body.

"My old man said he worked you over good. He said you know what time it is now."

Rudy glanced at the clock on the gym wall. "He's right—it's 9:15, Maury. See?" Rudy narrowed his eyes behind his glasses. "Now dry up, would you?"

Once more, he started toward his place in the inspection line, and again Maury got in his path with his hulking form. Rudy tried not to gulp. He tried to concentrate on the large pimple on Maury's chin.

"My old man wasn't just giving you the business, see?" Maury said. "He means what he says. Lay off me and my sister or there's gonna be trouble. And that goes for your sister and that other kid, too."

Rudy gathered what little courage he had left and forced himself to put his hand up on Maury's shoulder. "You know, it's too bad, Maury."

"What is?"

"That you couldn't handle it on your own. That you had to

have your daddy come running over to stand up for you."

Rudy gave the shoulder a pat, and this time he succeeded in getting past him to the line. It took that long for Maury to figure out what had just been said to him.

By that time, Coach had tooted his whistle and class began. Although Maury shot as many dark looks at Rudy as he did basketballs, there wasn't a chance for him to pick up with Rudy where he'd left off.

But Rudy knew it wasn't over. He knew that Mr. Worthington's threat had only made Maury feel like he could do whatever he wanted to Rudy. And Rudy knew he would.

He was right. The minute Rudy got his clothes off to get into the shower after gym class, Maury leaped out from behind a large trash can and picked Rudy up, throwing him, naked, over his shoulder.

"Hey, put me down!" Rudy yelled.

"I will—out in the hall!"

There was a chorus of raucous laughter as a crowd gathered to follow them to the door.

"Wait, no!" Rudy screamed.

Maury stopped. "Oh, I get it," he said. "You need your glasses, right, Four Eyes?"

"Somebody get his glasses for him!" another voice cried.

Chaos broke loose as part of the gym class dove for Rudy's bag and the other half charged ahead to open the door with Rudy shouting above all of them until he thought his lungs would burst.

The confusion was broken open by the blast of a whistle. Maury dropped Rudy to the floor, and everyone scattered.

"What's going on, Hutchinson?" Coach said.

"Nothing, sir," Rudy said, and he dove, red-faced and shaking, for the shower.

By the time the school day was over, Rudy was so exhausted from constantly looking over his shoulder for Maury, he could barely get through his deliveries for the bakery. And as he dragged in when he was finished, Ingrid's smirk didn't help.

But when he got home, Rudy sat right down in the library to work on his book report so that when Dad arrived, he would see him being studious and would maybe go easier on the punishment for last night's escapade. Still, it didn't seem fair somehow. Mr. Ness had been right: *This time* he'd only been trying to help.

When Dad finally arrived, however, he didn't seem to notice *what* Rudy was doing. Nor did he react to the fact that Little Al slipped in just behind him. He just sat the three kids down in the library again, and this time he seemed to have control of himself once more.

"I've given this a lot of thought," he said.

"Uh-oh," Little Al mumbled.

"And I think most of the fault for what is happening with you children lies, as usual, with me. I haven't given you a *chance* to be children, and I'm going to make up for that."

"But what if I don't want to be a child?" Hildy Helen said. "What if I want to be a—"

"Let the man finish, would ya, Dollface?" Little Al said.

Yeah, Rudy thought. *This has got to be better than a week in my room!*

Dad continued. "This Friday night, I am going to take all of you to the Riverview Amusement Park. It's October already. They'll be closing for the season soon, and I haven't taken you all summer. It will do us all good—you three, LaDonna, her friend—what's her name?"

"Ingrid?" Rudy said.

"Is that the one she's been studying with so hard?"

"Yes," Hildy Helen said, with her bottom lip stuck out.

Why does she *have to come?* Rudy thought.

"If you don't mind, I think I'll stay here and give Quintonia an evening to herself," Miss Tibbs said from the library doorway. "The last time I rode on a roller coaster, let's just say it wasn't pretty."

"And I hear they have *six* of them there!" Hildy Helen said.

One for every one of your emotions, Rudy thought. And he sighed. At least Miss Tibbs wasn't coming.

"All right then. It's settled," Dad said. "Hildy Helen, you are excused. Al, would you wait for me outside the door? I'd like to speak with you alone."

"Sure, Mr. Hutchie," Little Al said.

He looked white-faced and meek as he hurried out of the room behind Hildy Helen. Rudy started to get up, but Dad pointed to the chair, and he sank back into it.

"We still have a little matter to discuss," he said.

Rudy tried not to groan. Instead, he prayed. *Jesus, please let him—let somebody—understand!*

"I understand what you were trying to do last night, son," Dad said. "And I also know my part in it. However, you acted on impulse, and I don't want that to happen again. I want you to learn to think things through a little more carefully. So—"

Rudy held his breath. *Please don't let him say I can't go Friday night. Please don't let him tell me I can't be in the Argosy Club. Please no bed without dinner. I'm so hungry!*

"I am going to ask you to help pay to replace the glass in my office door."

"Pay?" Rudy said. He was surprised he got that much out. His face was going stiff.

"You have a job. I think two weeks' pay would be a sufficient contribution. What is that, a dollar and a half?"

"But—"

"I know you'll want extra money for our night at Riverview, so you can wait two weeks from this Friday to pay me. Keep whatever Oscar pays you this week. I'm trying not to be unreasonable."

"But—"

Dad's eyes grew smaller behind his glasses. "You don't think this is fair?"

Rudy clamped his mouth shut and shook his head. *What good is it going to do me to argue?* he thought. *I'm never going to get my stuff in the Argosy magazine anyway, so what difference does it make?*

It was hard to look forward to Friday now, but when it finally came around, Sylvia once more gave Rudy a dollar for his week's pay. With a slightly lighter heart, Rudy tucked it into his pocket and vowed not to spend it at the amusement park. At least he would have something to give to Van on Monday.

There was an early October crispness in the air as Dad, Hildy Helen, Rudy, Little Al, LaDonna, and Ingrid piled out of the Pierce Arrow at Riverview that evening, and there was a colorful crowd there to enjoy it. The merry-go-round, the Ferris wheel, and the six wooden-framed roller coasters Hildy Helen had predicted were all alive with people having a childlike good time.

As they stood in a crowded line while Dad purchased tickets, Rudy looked around at the arcade booths filled with huge stuffed animals. Barkers called out, "Try this game of skill! You could be a winner!" The smell of popcorn and hot dogs surrounded him, as did a crush of people who crowded around to try their hands at the games. He looked at the rides, towering over the park and operated by unshaven young men. Kids dashed from one ride to another, dragging teddy bears their fathers had won for them in the arcade. Rudy noticed a couple in their twenties darting through the crowd with ice cream teetering on cones, squealing as shrilly as any of the kids.

Rudy felt a strange stab of sadness. *They act like they don't have any problems at all*, he thought. *That's the way Dad wants us to act, but I can't.*

The idea that perhaps he would never be able to again—that he could never be carefree or play another prank or lay all his troubles out for Aunt Gussie to help him solve—brought on the pressure like he'd never felt it before.

And now, there was nothing he could do to relieve it.

"What are we going on first?" Hildy Helen said. She was looking from one roller coaster to another and doing a dance in front of Dad.

"Aeroplane swing!" Little Al said. "No, the shooting gallery!"

"Bobs!" LaDonna said.

"Flying Twins!" said Ingrid.

"Me, too!" Hildy Helen cried.

"I was kind of thinking about the gorilla show," Rudy said.

"No!" everyone shouted.

"I have a plan," Dad said. "We'll all go on the Ferris wheel, and from the top we'll be able to see the whole park. We can decide from there."

"I love the way lawyers think," Ingrid said.

The three girls held hands as the whole group ran shouting to the Ferris wheel and crowded into another line. Rudy looked up and gave a shiver.

"It sure is high," Hildy Helen said, as if she'd read his mind.

"Yeah, but you'll be in one a them cages," Little Al said.

Which was true. The Ferris wheel was made up of large meshed-in "cages" that swung happily as the wheel made its circle over Chicago. The only way to fall out of one was to open the door and practically jump.

"One more car and then we're up," Ingrid said as they inched forward in the line. She turned to Rudy. "No funny business, Hutchinson—no rocking or any of that. I get seasick, and I'd hate to throw up on you."

That's a surprise, Rudy said to himself. *I thought I'd be the first person she'd want to—*

"Next!" said the Ferris wheel operator.

They all turned toward the boy in the shirt with wide stripes. "Oh," LaDonna said, "I thought there was one more car before us."

"It just went," the kid said. He was the kind who seemed to say everything as if someone had just insulted him.

"Well, come on then!" Little Al said. "Where's Mr. Hutchie?"

They all looked around, but Dad was nowhere in sight.

"Hey, are you gettin' on or not?" Striped Shirt said.

"As soon as we find Mr. Hutchinson," LaDonna told him primly.

"Guy about this tall, wavy hair, glasses? Was standin' here with you a minute ago?"

They gave a unanimous nod.

Striped Shirt pointed to the car that was now swinging upward on the wheel. "He just got in that cage with a coupla fellas in fedoras. Who'd put on the Ritz to come to an amusement park is beyond me, but—"

"LaDonna!" Rudy said. His heart was already pounding over the happy squeals of the Ferris wheel riders. "That had to be the Mob! They've got Dad!"

Chapter Thirteen

I ngrid folded her arms across her chest. "The last time you thought the Mob had your father, Hutchinson," she said, "you ended up throwing a vase at a federal agent!"

"Rudy, really," LaDonna said. "I'm tired of your tricks—"

"Leave him alone!"

They all turned to look at Hildy Helen, who had her hands on her hips and was stomping the ground with one foot.

"If Rudy says Dad's in trouble, then he is! I know that look in his eyes."

Ingrid peered closely at Rudy. "What look?"

"Are you getting on or not?" Striped Shirt said.

"Yeah," Little Al said, and he caught Rudy and Hildy Helen by their shirt sleeves and dragged them toward the waiting cage. "The Mob musta tailed us here."

"All right, you keep them in sight," LaDonna said. "We'll find a policeman—just in case."

"Have you gone crazy, too, LaDonna?" Ingrid said.

But their voices melted into the crowd as Little Al, Hildy Helen, and Rudy climbed into the cage and Striped Shirt slammed the mesh-covered door.

"No clownin' around up there," Striped Shirt said. "I'm gonna be watchin' you—just like I'm watchin' them three up there."

He pointed to the car ahead of them, which Rudy was sure two mobsters had just shoved his father into. It was rocking crazily.

"Mr. Hutchie's puttin' up a good fight," Little Al said as their cage swung forward. "Keep fightin', Mr. Hutchie," he added through tightened teeth. "We're comin'."

"What do you mean, we're coming?" Rudy said.

But Little Al was already examining the clasp on the cage door. "All right, soon as we get to the top where we're above 'em, we climb out and jump down to the top a their cage."

"What?" Hildy Helen and Rudy said together.

"That'll get their attention on us, and they'll leave Mr. Hutchie alone. That is, if it ain't too late."

"What do you mean too late?" Hildy Helen said. Her usually rosy-cheeked face was going green.

"Never mind," Rudy said quickly. "He's right. It's the only way we can get to Dad. Do you know how to get the door open, Al?"

Little Al, of course, did. And as the car crept and rocked its way to the top of the Ferris wheel, he gave the twins their instructions. "All ya gotta do is back out and hang on tight right here." He tapped the edge of the doorway. "Then ya just drop onto the cage under us. By that time, it'll be Mr. Hutchie's."

Rudy and Hildy Helen both nodded. Rudy knew his face was pulled as tight as Hildy Helen's stockings. But she didn't look half as scared. Her mouth was set in a line, the way Dad's was when he was determined to make something happen, no matter what. It crossed Rudy's mind, crazily, that she was afraid about boys, but she sure loved a hair-raising adventure.

"All right, here goes," Little Al said. The cage door opened.

Jesus? Rudy prayed, heart racing. *Please let me be wrong. Please let this all be a mistake. Please—don't let Dad be in trouble.*

Please help us!

The cage rocked sharply, and suddenly all he could see of Little Al were his hands, white-knuckled around the door ledge. And then they were gone.

Hildy Helen peered out. "He made it! I'm going, Rudy. Be careful!"

And then she, too, was nothing but a set of fingers clinging to a Ferris wheel cage. Rudy felt sick. He tried to get the attention of the boy in the striped shirt to stop the ride. But no one could hear his yelling over the loud engine that spun the cages around the huge wheel.

"Come on, Rudy!" he heard Hildy Helen call to him. "It's easy!"

He forced himself to look down as the cage continued its downward curve with Dad's cage just below them. Little Al was already halfway upside down, looking inside, and Hildy Helen was on her knees looking up at Rudy. They were at least a hundred feet in the air.

"Come on! It's just another trick!" Hildy called to him.

Rudy's stomach turned, and he shook his head. The cage swung crazily.

"Come *on*!" she cried. "Just pretend it's fun! You'll do anything for fun!"

Suddenly it didn't matter that what she was saying made no sense at all. Just her saying it—the way nobody else would think to say it—made him turn around and back slowly out of the cage.

"Now just hold on with your hands and let go with everything else!" Hildy Helen shouted.

At that point, she wasn't the only one shouting. There was a holler from below that could only have come from the surly mouth of Striped Shirt. Help couldn't be far away.

So Rudy let go "with everything but his hands." Just as he did, the Ferris wheel lurched to a stop and Rudy swung, legs dangling, fingers barely hanging on, far above the city of Chicago.

"Let go!" Hildy Helen shouted.

Other voices from below were by now calling, "Hang on! Don't let go!"

But Rudy only heard Hildy Helen's. He forced himself to uncurl his fingers and dropped. He nearly cried when his feet hit the top of the cage below.

But there was no time for crying. Little Al was on his stomach, head hanging down so that he could see into the cage, even as the Ferris wheel started up again.

"Is it Dad?" Hildy shouted.

"Al, get away," Dad shouted back, but then his voice was cut off.

But Rudy didn't think past that. His prayer hadn't been answered. He hadn't been wrong.

The cage was now about halfway down the other side. Rudy searched for signs of LaDonna and Ingrid and a policeman. All he saw were people pointing and screaming—and even smiling. It was as if Rudy and Little Al and Hildy Helen were providing the latest thrill for a crowd that any minute would move restlessly on to look for the next one.

"Get a policeman!" Rudy called to them.

If they even heard him he never knew. For suddenly Striped Shirt brought the Ferris wheel to an abrupt halt again about 20 feet from the ground, and the cage door flew open. Rudy saw his father's gray woolen trouser leg appear and hang in mid-air.

Little Al thrust a hand down into the cage and came out with a black fedora. Its satiny white lining shone in the Ferris wheel's lights.

"Hey!" a harsh voice from inside shouted.

It was almost in unison with Striped Shirt, who was now more than insulted at the shenanigans happening on his wheel.

"Get us down—fast!" Rudy shouted to him. For the mobster's plan was suddenly as clear in his head as one of his drawings: They were going to shove Dad out while they were still high enough to hurt him.

If Striped Shirt could just get the cage too low for it to do them any good before they—

"Hurry!" Hildy Helen screamed at the operator.

The Ferris wheel seemed to go into higher gear, and the cage plunged toward the ground. Another leg thrust through the open door—this one clad in cuffed black trousers—and then another. A big-shouldered man with hair thick with Vaseline hurled himself out of the cage. Another man came after him, clutching their father by the back of his natty sweater.

The crowd screamed like one thrilled person as the three tumbled to the ground, rolled, and then disappeared as if they had been swallowed up by the band of sensation-seekers.

The ground was quickly coming closer, and Rudy barely noticed when Little Al gave him a shove toward it and he dropped the last six feet. By the time Rudy was scrambling to his feet, Ingrid and LaDonna were there, breathless and wild-eyed.

"What was *that* all about, Hutchinson?" Ingrid said. "Are you *completely* out of your mind? You could have been killed."

"I know, but it was the only way—" Rudy answered.

"It was the Mob!" Hildy Helen cried. "Just like Rudy said it was!"

"They got Mr. Hutchie," Little Al said. "Where's the cops?"

LaDonna shook her head. "There isn't a policeman or a telephone in this whole place. And I think you're right about the Mob. There's a man parked in a car outside the front gate with the motor running. I've seen him outside the law office, too."

"That could just be protection Mr. Ness has hired for your father," Ingrid said.

LaDonna shook her head again. "Then he'd be in here protecting him, not out there."

"Would you dolls dummy up?" Little Al's dark eyes were flashing. "We gotta get to Mr. Hutchie before they—"

"Don't say it!" Hildy Helen said, clapping her hands over her ears. "Let's just find him!"

Through it all, Rudy's mind had been spinning. *It's just another trick. Pretend it's fun.* That was what Hildy Helen had said. His head was clear now, working like a prankster's.

"All right," he said, "if that fella is out there with the motor running, that means they're still in the park someplace. LaDonna, you go watch the car. We'll split up and look in all the places where they could—well, that they would—"

"We get the idea," Ingrid said. "Forget the merry-go-round. Check the roller coasters."

"Gotcha!" Little Al said. And grabbing Hildy Helen's wrist, he took off.

"Come on, Hutchinson," Ingrid said. "Let's get a wiggle on. If anybody's fast, it's you."

There was no time to wonder what she meant by that. Rudy charged across the park, in the opposite direction from the one Hildy Helen and Little Al had taken. "You look that way, I'll look this way. But we stay close to each other—"

"Hutchinson!" Ingrid had come to a stop and was pointing. "There they are!"

Rudy took off running before it even registered where she was sending them.

"The Tunnel of Love?" Ingrid said breathlessly as they ran. "These hoodlums are blooey. But that's just my opinion."

A clump of people chose that moment to stop in front of them and examine their popcorn. Rudy lost sight of the thugs and Dad.

"Look out!" Rudy shouted at them and shouldered his way through them, sending their snack in all directions.

They hollered indignantly, but Rudy charged on—in time to see the man who still had his hat drop a large wad of bills into the Tunnel operator's hand. By the time Rudy and Ingrid got there, Dad and his two captors had disappeared inside.

Rudy elbowed in front of a waiting rider and said, "We gotta have the next boat."

But the operator shook his head. He, too was wearing a striped shirt, and had the same insulted look on his face. "You see this?" he said, holding out what must have been several hundred dollars. "They paid me not to let any more boats go in. I don't cross fellas like that."

"I got money, too!" Rudy said, and pulled the dollar out of his knickers pocket.

"Oh, for crying out loud!" Ingrid said. "Get in, Rudy!"

She gave Rudy a shove toward a waiting boat and was hauling it ahead by pushing her hands along the side of the tunnel before Rudy could get all the way in.

"Hey, you can't do that!" the operator shouted.

"So call a cop!" Rudy shouted back.

They sank into the darkness of the tunnel, and Rudy peered into it. Somehow even in the midst of the last half hour's acrobatics, his glasses had managed to stay on his face.

"Can you see them?" Ingrid said.

"No—yes!" Rudy said.

They had just rounded a bend, and three silhouettes cut sharply into the light from the other end of the tunnel. One wore a fedora. One had wavy hair that seemed to bush out in fear. One was holding something long to Wavy Hair's head. And this time Rudy knew it wasn't a cigar.

"No!" Rudy cried.

The head with the fedora swung around, and a curse echoed through the tunnel. The gun pulled away from Dad's head and pointed straight at Rudy.

"Get down!" Rudy shouted.

The boat lurched back and forth as both he and Ingrid flattened themselves against its bottom. Rudy squeezed his eyes shut and waited for the crack he'd heard too many times before. Instead, he heard only a voice shouting from the other end of the tunnel.

"Police!" it said. "Come outta that tunnel with yer hands up!"

Rudy knew who it was. The thugs obviously didn't. As Rudy brought his head up from the bottom of the boat, they were hauling Dad out of their boat and sloshing with him back toward the entrance. Rudy threw himself back to the bottom until they were past.

"Keep them in sight, Hutchinson," Ingrid whispered to him. "I'll tell the cops at the other end."

Rudy didn't have time to tell her the "cops" were just Little Al. He, too, jumped out of the boat and splashed through the knee-deep water out of the tunnel. The operator sat lazily at his post, flipping through his money. Dad and the mobsters were ahead, disappearing into the crowd toward the park entrance.

By the time Rudy got to the gate, LaDonna was near tears.

"They're putting him in that car!" she said. "We have got to find the police!"

"Leave the park and call 'em!" Rudy said. "Little Al knows how to get into a call box. I'll follow Dad!"

Before LaDonna could protest, Rudy was off again, tearing out of the gate. But the car with his father in it was already pulling away.

If anybody's fast, it's you, Ingrid had said. But Rudy knew he wasn't fast enough to keep up with a Lincoln going 25 miles an hour. His heart began to pound painfully in his ears again.

Jesus, please! he prayed. *I'm not fooling around. This is real! Please, I have to save my dad!*

And then he saw a way. A taxi was approaching, its yellow paint job gleaming in the streetlights and its running board jutting out. The image of a man, riding on a running board as he careened down Michigan Avenue what seemed like so long ago, now leaped to the center of Rudy's mind. Coiling up for the spring, he waited—and jumped on.

"Hey, no free rides, kid!" the driver shouted from inside.

"I got money!" Rudy shouted back and pulled the dollar bill from his pocket.

"Then get in!"

"No time! Just follow that black Lincoln!"

Maybe it had been a slow night for the taxi driver. Maybe he was one of those sensation-seekers. Or maybe it was just the answer to Rudy's prayers. Whatever it was, the driver gunned the engine, and the taxi leaped forward with Rudy hanging onto the door handle for his life.

Chapter Fourteen

*T*he taxi driver seemed to be having the time of his life, weaving in and out of the light evening traffic after the Lincoln. Rudy, however, was sweating so badly he was afraid his hands would slip off the handle and he'd land in the street while the mobsters took his father who knew where.

But it quickly became apparent "where." They were headed for the river, winding their way toward the Chicago Street Bridge, and it made Rudy shiver through his sweat. He'd been down here only once delivering doughnuts. Not many people ordered baked goods in this part of town where the alleys always seemed to be damp and gloomy and the out-of-work set skulked in their shadows. Rudy's heart had beat a little harder when he'd wheeled through here on his bicycle. Right now it was threatening to pound right out of his chest.

There was no one there that night except the men in the Lincoln, and Rudy and his taxi driver. The Lincoln drove off the side of Chicago Street at the river and headed under the bridge. Rudy stopped his driver.

"Thanks for the lift," he said, tossing his dollar bill through the open window.

"You gonna be all right, kid?" the driver said. "What are you gettin' into, anyway?"

"I gotta help my dad. Could you get me a policeman?"

"A what? Hey, what is this, kid?"

But Rudy didn't answer. He could hear car doors slamming under the bridge, and he ran toward them.

The Lincoln was parked beside the first pillar of the bridge that was still on dry land, and Rudy hid behind it. From there, he could see the two men hauling his father up the slope toward the bridge itself. Dad's hands were tied behind his back, and there was a rag stuffed in his mouth.

You're a rat, Jim Hutchinson. This is what happens to rats. Mark it.

Mark it. Rudy suddenly remembered what Little Al had said that meant. "'Don't you forget it,'"Al had told him. "When a mobster says mark something, that means it's gonna happen."

No, it isn't! Rudy's mind screamed. *Jesus, please help me! Don't let this happen!*

As soon as the men reached the bridge, Rudy scrambled from his hiding place and, being careful to stay in the shadows, followed them up. He stayed toward the bottom, about 10 feet from where the two men stopped and tied a rope around Dad's ankles. He was squirming and making muffled sounds through his gag, but they bound him up as if he were a rag doll and carried him by his elbows toward the top of the bridge.

If Dad couldn't get away from them, Rudy thought, what could he do to stop them? Panic was rising in his stomach, and he looked around wildly. Had the taxi driver gotten the police? Or had he, too, thought Rudy was nothing but a prankster?

But even as Rudy whipped his head around in terror, his eye caught on something. It wasn't the police, but it was the next best thing.

"Hey, you! Stop! Police!" he yelled in his deepest voice. He knew he didn't sound a thing like Detective Zorn or even Little Al, but it startled the men enough to stop them at the railing. Rudy tore like a racehorse to the green call box he'd spotted on a pole and dug into his pocket for something—anything—that he could use to pry it open.

There was nothing.

Rudy searched the ground frantically, his mind thinking crazily, *Where's a hairpin?*

There was nothing that even remotely resembled one. Rudy balled his hand into a fist and pounded it against the call box. Behind him on the bridge he could hear the men's clipped voices, bickering back and forth.

"Wasn't no cop—"

"Just do it—"

"So long, rat—"

The noise of Rudy's heart beating in his ear pounded out the rest—along with his own voice screaming, "No! Don't push him! No!" as he tore toward the top of the bridge.

And then there was another sound: the high-pitched whine of a siren.

The men heard it, too, for they froze with Dad between them. Then it was as if time slowed down. Rudy was hauling as fast as he could, but his legs dragged. The men took a long look at each other and then at Dad. The siren stretched out in a never-ending wail.

And then things sprang to life again, and the two men lifted Rudy's father and tossed him like a bag of garbage into the Chicago River.

They were gone before Rudy heard the splash. Rudy never saw them. He was already tearing the six feet to the bottom of the bridge and then under it and into the water from the bank. It was cold, and it was green-black, and it smelled of algae, but Rudy cut through it with his arms, legs thrashing behind him, calling his father's name as the water rushed in his face.

"Dad!" Rudy sputtered. "Dad, where are you?"

But tied up and unable to move so much as an arm, Jim Hutchinson was nowhere in sight on the surface of the water.

Rudy dove under and opened his eyes, but the river was so murky he could barely see his own hand in front of his face. He felt around in a frenzy until his lungs threatened to tear open. When he came up to gasp for air, he could hear voices from the bank, but he didn't care. Let the Mob come back for him. They were going to find him still looking for his father.

He went under again and strained to see. There was some kind of light coming from above now—just enough to reveal a dark shape below and in front of him. Rudy grabbed for it and felt something give. Then his fingers touched rope, and he knew it was Dad.

Rudy was running out of air, but he didn't let go of his father as he struggled for the surface. Dad was like a dead weight in Rudy's grasp, but with his own face just barely above the water, Rudy grabbed him with both hands so that at least his nose could get breath. The rag in his mouth was soaked, and the water from it ran right into Dad's nostrils as he tilted his head back to breathe.

Rudy snatched the rag out, and his father choked and spluttered until his face darkened.

"Hold on, Dad!" Rudy cried, barely able to speak above a cough himself.

Dad nodded, but he couldn't hold on, not with his hands tied. He could do nothing but let Rudy try to tow him toward the bank. Rudy treaded himself around so he could see how far they had to go. He gasped at what he saw.

The riverbank was a mass of cars with their headlights pointed toward the river. There were no sirens now, just the shouts of the men peering out into the river.

"There! I see him!" one of them called out.

"I see two heads! Hold on out there! We're coming to get you!"

Rudy did, as a man's body hit the water and swam toward them, arms chopping the river like a machine.

"Please, Jesus," Rudy prayed. "Don't let it be one of them."

At last a prayer was answered. The swimmer was Detective Zorn.

By the time they reached Prairie Avenue, completely dried out and totally filled with hot cocoa and thoroughly questioned by Detective Zorn, another police car had brought LaDonna, Ingrid, Hildy Helen, and Little Al home. Oscar had arrived, too, to try to coax them all to eat oatmeal cookies while they'd paced the floor and taken turns waiting at the window.

Quintonia enfolded both Dad and a very numb Rudy into her arms and wouldn't let them go until Hildy Helen pried them apart. Even LaDonna refused to wait for her turn but squeezed herself in and held Rudy against her while Miss Tibbs took over with Dad.

"I thought we'd lost you both," LaDonna said. "I couldn't have stood it."

"I wanna know what happened," Little Al said.

"Every detail," Hildy Helen said. "And don't skip anything."

Miss Tibbs let go of Dad long enough to help Quintonia produce a pot of tea to go with the oatmeal cookies. Still, no one ate as Rudy and Dad pieced the story together for them. When they were finished, Oscar shook his gray head.

"I always knew you were something special, liebschen," he said to Rudy. "I always knew."

"What's a 'liebschen'"? Hildy Helen said.

Oscar began to hold forth. Ingrid nudged Rudy, and he looked at her.

"I guess I was wrong about you, Hutchinson," she whispered. "And my father was right."

Rudy shrugged, and his face burned, and he stuffed a whole cookie into his mouth. It was a huge relief when Oscar said, "Come on, Inky. We have to go home. This is too much excitement for me."

"It's too much excitement for *anyone*," Miss Tibbs said. "I suggest we all go to bed. I'm going to invite myself to sleep on the sofa, if you don't mind."

Rudy didn't object, even to himself. He couldn't think about anything except that just a few hours before, he had watched two men throw his father to what was supposed to be his death. As Rudy lay in bed, even after Little Al had fallen into an exhausted sleep, he couldn't close his eyes without the picture appearing before him. The men binding Dad up like a bundle of newspapers, hauling him to the top of the bridge, hurling him over the railing, and wanting him to die.

Rudy began to shake. He pulled another blanket over him, but he still shivered, from the inside out. Little Al churned restlessly, and Rudy got out of bed and tiptoed out, hugging his arms around himself. His palms were clammy even through the sleeves of his pajamas.

As he crept down the stairs, the shadows in the front hall looked suddenly evil, like long hands stretching out to pull Dad into a Ferris wheel only to push him off; to yank Dad into a Tunnel of Love, only to point a gun at his head; to carry Dad to the top of a bridge, only to—

Rudy put his hands over his face and felt them tremble against his cheeks. It was all over. Dad was safe here in the house.

But the fear still held onto Rudy, and it wouldn't let go.

There was a sound from down the hall, past the library, and Rudy jumped. But it was only Aunt Gussie moaning. Rudy went toward the library to find a lap blanket and snuggle in among the familiar books and papers and maybe stop shaking.

Aunt Gussie moaned again, and Rudy heard snoring. Either Miss Tibbs was cutting Zs on the sitting room sofa, or Quintonia was so exhausted she was asleep in her chair outside Aunt Gussie's door.

A peek down the hall revealed Quintonia, head lolling over the side of the chair, deep sounds gurgling from her throat. Inside the room, Aunt Gussie still moaned.

It upsets her every time she hears your voice, Quintonia had told him.

Rudy almost reached out to shake Quintonia. Aunt Gussie obviously needed something. But the moan seemed to change. It wasn't just a shapeless groan anymore. Rudy was sure it was saying, "Ru—Ru—"

Rudy wiped the scared sweat off his upper lip and silently pushed open the bedroom door.

There was a soft light coming from a lamp on the bedside table, and in its glow Rudy could see Aunt Gussie, struggling to pull herself up in her bed. When she saw Rudy, her good hand came out, and she pointed a shaking finger at him.

"All right," Rudy whispered. "I'll leave. I just thought you wanted something."

"Ru!" she said. And she pointed harder.

"You want me?" Rudy said.

Aunt Gussie nodded and fell back against the pillows as if the whole "conversation" had worn her out. Rudy padded to her and stood by the bed. She pointed to it. Rudy sat down.

He was on her left side, so that she had to turn her face against the pillow to see him. Her left side was lost in its billows, and at once she looked like the old Aunt Gussie. Her good eye was studying him, and Rudy knew she was seeing everything.

"Ru," she said, shaking her head. She put out her hand, and Rudy put his in it. She squeezed, and he was surprised at how strong it was. Rudy clung to it, and she clung back.

"Ru," she said again. She looked down at Rudy's clammy palm and wiped it off with her fingertips. When she looked back up at him, there was a question in her eye.

"Yeah, I'm still scared," Rudy said. "Did Quintonia tell you what happened?"

Aunt Gussie nodded.

"Eliot Ness came to the police station when we were there, and he told Dad he already has a 24-hour watch out in front of the house, and somebody will follow Dad around all the time."

She gave a soft moan.

"And Dad said it's the first time he ever felt like there might really be an end to the Mob rule here in Chicago."

She moaned again.

"But I'm still scared, Aunt Gussie. I guess I'm a sissy, but I can't help it. I keep shaking and thinking the shadows are alive. I'm just so scared inside."

"Ru." She was pointing to the bedside table, where Rudy saw there was a pad of paper and a small silver pencil.

"You want that?" Rudy said.

She nodded, and Rudy handed them to her. Aunt Gussie motioned for him to hold the pad still while she wrote.

It wasn't Aunt Gussie's usual perfect penmanship, but Rudy could read it. It said: *Of course, you're afraid.*

"But I'm supposed to not act like a kid now. Only sometimes I am supposed to. I don't know what to do anymore!"

Aunt Gussie shook her head and wrote some more. *I'm afraid, too. If that's what you are, that's what you are.*

"I don't like it," Rudy said. "And I know I can't chase it away doing pranks."

She shook her head so firmly, Rudy expected her to give him a tongue lashing, too. She was so much like the old Aunt Gussie now. Rudy leaned forward.

"So what do I *do*, Aunt Gussie? I tried just having fun so I wouldn't feel like I was going to explode, but that didn't work. I tried to work hard and do everything right, and half the time that doesn't work either. I can't even do anything right with Hildy Helen, and she's my twin sister! Everything's awful! I can't be in the Argosy Club, I have to pay for the window, Maury Worthington is after me, I think Little Al's going bad again, maybe, and Dad doesn't seem to be doing anything about it—and I'm so scared. I'm just so scared, Aunt Gussie!"

She put her hand up to his face, and Rudy couldn't hold back any longer. He exploded into tears—big sobs—with his face on her bed. He cried until he fell asleep.

When he woke up, Aunt Gussie was sleeping, too, with her hand against his cheek. On the covers beside him was a note she had written.

Rudolph, it said. *You've done all you can. Just pray now, and wait on the Lord. He will take care of you in spite of you. GN*

Rudy folded the note and took it upstairs and tucked it into the pocket of his knickers. Even as he climbed into bed, trembling again, he wasn't sure it would help, but he closed his eyes, and when the vision of the bridge flickered on, he whispered, "I'm waiting on You, Jesus. Please take care of me in spite of me." He fell asleep still murmuring those words.

Chapter Fifteen

*F*or the next week, Rudy did almost nothing when he wasn't
in school except draw prayers and sit with Aunt Gussie.
She didn't write him any more notes. They mostly just sat. But he
looked at the one she'd given him at least 10 times a day. If he did-
n't, he found himself sweating and shivering and on the edge of
tears all at the same time.

Dad gave his formal testimony before Eliot Ness's commission.
After that, he spent every evening with the children and LaDonna.
Miss Tibbs did, too. So did the police bodyguard, who followed them
everywhere. They went to Grant Park for ice cream and frankfurters.
They went to the Biograph Theatre and saw Al Jolson in *Say It With
Songs*. They sat on a wall down by Lake Michigan and watched a V
of Canada geese fly over them, so close they could see their feet
tucked up under them.

"Are you gonna draw that?" Little Al said. "Them feet curled up
there like that?"

Rudy shrugged.

"I would if I could draw like you," Hildy Helen said. "I heard
boys like girls who are artistic."

"Yeah, I like a doll that can draw," Little Al said after careful thought.

LaDonna poked Rudy with a pink fingernail. "How's that book report coming?" she said.

"I read the book," Rudy said.

"Did you like it?"

"Yeah, it was Bible stories, only in poems."

"I know," LaDonna said. "It's my favorite book. It inspires me. But you haven't written the report?"

"I don't know what to write," Rudy said. His heart was starting to beat fast again, and his mouth was going dry. He didn't even have to look at his hands to know they were sweating. "It won't matter what I write anyway. Mr. Keating won't like it. He hates me."

"So don't write it," LaDonna said. "Draw it."

"He's not gonna let me get away with that! He already thinks I'm the class clown."

"Just draw until you get an idea to write," LaDonna said. "You have to use what you can do and who you are, Rudy. You did that the other night."

"What other night?"

"When you saved your father's life! You used all the same clever ideas you would have used if you'd been up to no good."

"I don't want to talk about it," Rudy said.

"Then don't," LaDonna said, sniffing. "Draw it."

Later that night, he discovered that drawing it was better than staring at a blank piece of paper and feeling the anxiety race through his veins like liquid barbed wire. So Rudy did draw that night. He drew a picture of Noah herding the animals onto the ark, looking back over his shoulder as the sky shook with thunder.

Huh, Rudy thought as he surveyed his finished product. *I can see the thunder.*

He could also see the fear in Noah's eyes. Somehow, it made his own fear settle down, just a little.

"There's one thing I forgot to tell you."

Rudy jumped. LaDonna was standing behind him, looking over his shoulder.

"I forgot to tell you," she said, "that it's taken me a long time to know what God wants from me. I had to study about it. That's me. You have to draw it. That's you. Hildy Helen has to dance it out. We're all different. But you have to let Him tell you through that. That's when I knew how to grow up—when I let Him tell me."

"But how?" Rudy said.

"Keep drawing," she said. She tapped Noah's face. "Draw some more fear."

And then she left.

It was at least a better week at the bakery than he'd ever had. A lot of his deliveries were made to the Chicago Mercantile Exchange on Washington and Franklin. Rudy quickly figured out that it was the stock market, and that the clerks and investors and stock brokers were living on doughnuts and sandwiches as they wrestled with a market that Dad said was going up and down like a roller coaster at the Riverview Amusement Park.

Ingrid left him alone most afternoons when he came back with his empty box. On Friday, though, she pulled him aside after Oscar had paid him his 75 cents and said, "Put out your hand."

"What are you gonna do?" Rudy said.

"Just because *you're* a trickster, Hutchinson, doesn't mean *I'm* in the habit of depositing live insects into people's hands. Come on, put it out there."

"I'm not a trickster anymore," Rudy said, and he held out his palm.

Ingrid dropped a shiny quarter onto it. "It isn't much, but I want you to have it. Kind of like a reward for how hard you've worked. I've been tough on you, and maybe you didn't deserve it."

Rudy looked up at her in surprise.

"You care a lot about people and about doing the right thing," she said. "Even when you try *not* to, you do it anyway."

"Me?" Rudy said.

"Look, I know it's hard being mature when other people aren't. I've been there. But if you stay with it and just wait, it'll be worth it, believe me. Being an only child, I always wished for a brother." She wrinkled her freckled nose. "So, maybe now I got one."

Rudy looked sadly at the quarter, for lack of anywhere else to look. "You don't want me for a brother. I can't even help the sister I got."

"You mean Hildy Helen—with her boy problems?"

Rudy nodded, and Ingrid laughed. "She's got it bad," she said, "but you can probably help her better than anybody, even me and LaDonna."

"I don't believe that," Rudy said.

"Well, that's just my opinion," Ingrid said, and she turned away. "Oh, and Hutchinson," she said, looking back at him over her shoulder. "Don't expect a tip like that quarter every Friday. I have college to pay for."

For almost the first time all week, Rudy smiled.

That night, Rudy turned a dollar and 25 cents over to his father. "For the window," he said. "I still owe you another quarter, but I'll get it next week, I promise."

Dad slowly folded the *Chicago Tribune* onto his lap and switched off Walter Winchell. "Rudy," he said, "I think I was too hard on you about the window. You don't have to pay for it. You were just trying to act grown-up and protect me."

But the fear of responsibility—of having to act like a grown-up and not being able to handle it all—started its race through Rudy's blood again. "I have to, Dad," he said. "I have to grow up right."

Dad nodded and took the money reverently from Rudy's hand. "I think you're on your way, son," he said. "You're closer than you think."

The fear slowed down some, just a little. Rudy went upstairs and drew some prayers and drew some poems and studied the frightened look around the prodigal son's mouth. The fear ebbed away a little more.

On Monday, Rudy turned in his book report on *God's Trombones*. It was three pages of writing and ten pages of drawings. Rudy's heart pounded as he handed it up the row. What was he going to do to keep the fear away without those drawings to do?

During activities period that day, Rudy stuck his hands in the empty pockets of his knickers and wandered over to the Games Club. A boy with smeared glasses looked up from a checkerboard.

"Does it cost anything to be in this club?" Rudy said.

The kid shook his head and went back to kinging his opponent.

"Hey, there, cutie!" said a voice behind him.

It was the bubbly ninth grader in a sweater with flowers embroidered all over it.

"What happened? Didn't you like the Argosy Club?"

"Yeah, I liked it fine," Rudy said. "I just—I don't know—"

"Van was mean to you, wasn't he?" Bubbles said. She planted her hands importantly on her hips. "He's such a big brute! Sometimes I'd just like to—"

She didn't finish telling whatever it was she wanted to do to the unsuspecting Van, but swished off, leaving Rudy sweaty-palmed beside the checker game.

Moments later, Van himself appeared at Rudy's side and steered him by the elbow to the Argosy Club's room. The place was dotted with students poring over writing tablets and sketch pads amid the stacks of *Argosy*s. Van stuck Rudy in a seat among them.

"What's up, kid?" Van said. "I thought you were running on all six cylinders. What happened?"

"I couldn't get the money," Rudy said. "Some other things came up and I had to use it—"

"Forget the dough! You're the best artist we got! Just sit down and start drawing, for Pete's sake."

A couple of the other kids looked up from their work and nodded.

But Rudy shook his head. "That wouldn't be right. Everybody else had to pay. It was my own fault anyway." He could hear his voice shaking, and he just wanted to "dummy up" and go hide.

"I never met a kid like you," Van said. "You're either completely blooey, or you're too responsible for your own good. I don't know which." He tossed his hair back. "All right, look. If you wander around out there the principal's going to collar you and all the responsibility in the world won't help you. Just stay in here and draw. And if you can't come up with the money by the time we go to press, we won't use any of your stuff if you don't want us to. Fair enough?"

Rudy's fingers suddenly ached for the feel of a drawing pencil. "All right," he said.

By the next Friday, he was 75 cents richer again, but Oscar's face looked slightly sad as he tucked the money into Rudy's hand.

"I don't know if you've noticed," Oscar said, "but business hasn't been so good lately—at least not as good as usual."

Rudy's stomach churned. "Are you letting me go?"

"No, no! Not yet! I'm going to keep you on as long as I can. I just want you to know if I do have to—it won't be your fault."

"You're a good boy," Sylvia chimed in from the cake counter.

Rudy started to leave, but an idea came to his head. "If it isn't going to be busy next week," he said, "could I bring my sister with me? You won't have to pay her or anything. She could just ride along with me, keep me company."

"Is she as smart as you?" Oscar said.

"Smarter."

"Then bring her along."

Rudy wasn't sure why he'd even asked for that. Hildy Helen was as up and down and in and out the last few weeks as she'd ever been. He just wanted to spend more time with his sister. Maybe what Ingrid had said was true; it had been running around in his head ever since: *You can probably help her better than anybody.*

But Rudy was even less sure about that when it took almost a week for Hildy Helen to agree to come with him. She listlessly watched Dorothea rake in notes from this boy and stroll down the hall with that boy and brag about still another boy at the lunch table, and every day Hildy Helen told Rudy, "I'm just too blue to go out."

Finally on Thursday, he was fed up. "I don't care what color you are!" he said. "You're goin' with me. Fellas don't like girls that moon around all the time."

She was out the door with him in five minutes.

And within another five minutes of wheeling away from the bakery with the box and the delivery instructions, Hildy Helen was laughing and staring wide-eyed as Rudy showed her some of his new discoveries.

"That's an Italian place," he told her on the corner of Wabash and 22nd Street. "All the show people go there—Caruso, Ziegfeld, lot of opera people, too."

"Do they eat doughnuts?"

"Nah. They buy their biscotti from Oscar."

"Biscotti from a German baker? Little Al would be insulted!"

Rudy shrugged happily. More of the fear of not being able to live up to his responsibilities was slipping away, just from being with his sister. She had a way about her.

They zipped through the deliveries, leaving plenty of time for Rudy to show Hildy the candy shops, the Victrola shops, the movie theaters they'd never even known existed before. Rudy even found himself looking up at the sky, which that day wore an even coat of gray paste, and around at the trees, ablaze with golds and reds. It might have been the first he'd even noticed much about his world since the day of Aunt Gussie's stroke.

But there was something different about the deliveries that day, October 24. Almost everywhere they went, people seemed to be glued to their radios, their faces long and some of them ashen. One woman took her loaf of bread and had to be reminded to pay, and her hands shook as she dug into her change purse. One man shouted at Rudy when he opened the door, "Get away! What do I want with pastries at a time like this?"

"You never told me people were so mean to you," Hildy Helen said.

"They usually aren't," Rudy said.

At their next stop, in the wealthy Northside where Rudy seldom went—because, as Oscar had once told him, the people there all had their own personal chefs to do their baking for them—Rudy listened carefully to the radio while the maid went off to get the money.

"A panic has broken out on the New York Stock Exchange," the speaker announced in a nearly breathless voice. "Prices on stocks have fallen an average of 18 points. Investors are scrambling to sell before prices fall still further. It looks as if the bottom has finally dropped out."

Rudy felt strange, as if some fortune-teller's prediction had just come true, and he couldn't be sure it was real. Aunt Gussie and Dad had been talking about a crash for over a year. Had it happened, and that was why so many people were wearing long faces and ignoring their eclairs?

He and Hildy Helen saw even more strange things as they walked their bikes back through the shady streets of the Northside. One man was walking out of his office building, mechanically tearing up a piece of paper into tinier and tinier pieces until it lay like confetti on the sidewalk. They saw a woman standing in the doorway of a broker's office, staring up at the screen and giggling worse than Hildy Helen *ever* had. But the saddest were those who simply sat and stared.

"Why does this matter so much?" Hildy Helen said as they passed yet another blinking, stony-faced man. A woman hurrying by with a pinched look on her own face stopped and looked at them so suddenly, the twins stopped, too.

"I'll tell you why it matters," the woman said. "Those numbers you see on those screens?"

The twins nodded.

"Those are the hopes of years being smashed, right before their eyes."

It sobered Hildy Helen and Rudy into silence for another block.

"Will Dad's hopes be smashed?" Hildy Helen said. "And Aunt Gussie's?"

"No," Rudy said. "They don't invest in the stock market."

"Oh," she said. She looked at him through a panel of her dark, bobbed hair. "You sure know a lot more than I do, Rudy. I think you're growing up faster than me."

Rudy looked away so she wouldn't see the fear run through his eyes. That was when they caught on a familiar figure.

He was sitting on a wooden box outside an elegant brownstone office building, shining the shoes of a man in a well-tailored suit whose face looked as if he'd just returned, dazed, from the war.

Beside him, Rudy heard Hildy Helen gasp.

"Rudy!" she said. "That shoe-shine boy! That's Little Al!"

She raised her hand as if to wave to him, but Rudy grabbed it and pushed her, bike and all, around the corner.

"What are you doing?" she said.

Rudy wasn't sure—until now. It all came to him in a rush, the way a picture did in his mind.

"Now I know where he's been going every day," Rudy said. "He's been out trying to make money, just like me."

"But why didn't he tell us?" Hildy Helen said.

Rudy knew that, too. "Don't you remember him saying he was going to get an education so he wouldn't have to shine shoes and sell two-cent papers like the other kids in Little Italy?"

"But there's no shame in that!"

"There is for him, because he thinks he's dumb."

Hildy Helen rolled her eyes. "He's no more dumb than you are a clown or I'm the bearcat of Hirsch Junior High."

Rudy squinted at her from behind his glasses. "Tell me again—what's a bearcat, anyway?"

"A girl that's pretty and fiery—"

"Oh, for crying out loud, Hildy Helen!" Rudy said. "You're 80 times prettier than that drip Dorothea—and you're the whole Chicago Fire next to her, next to any girl in that school! They're all—birthday candles compared to you!"

"Then why don't the boys like me the way they do her?"

"They *don't* like her!"

"But they walk down the hall with her and—"

"Because she *makes* them!" Rudy said. "I know the looks on their faces, Hildy Helen. They look like she's their mother and she's draggin' them to look at *dresses* or something! I don't know any fella in the seventh grade that wants to have some girl stuck on them—or stuck *to* them. It's only the girls that want that stuff. You just have to wait until it's time."

"Really? You're not just giving me the business?"

"No."

Hildy Helen blinked at him. "Then why didn't you ever tell me?" she said.

"Oh, brother," Rudy said.

Little Al was right. They could be thankful they weren't girls.

✢ ✢ ✢

*T*hat night, Miss Tibbs served hamburger sandwiches and Eskimo Pies, and it was the best thing she'd fixed for them since she'd taken over Quintonia's kitchen.

"You should make this every night," Rudy said. "Could I have another sandwich?"

"Save at least one for Little Al," Dad said.

Rudy and Hildy Helen looked at each other and smiled. Dad seemed to be smiling to himself, too.

Little Al must have told him what he was doing, Rudy thought. More and more things were making sense now. It was making the fear of figuring out how to grow up seem not quite so bad.

Not everything was fine, though. Dad was still in danger from the Mob. And Rudy still had the problem of how he was going to learn to do the right thing without playing pranks on everyone.

When Little Al finally got home, Dad was explaining what had happened on the stock market that day.

"The prices have been dropping over the last month or so," he said. "So a lot of those investors that had bought their stock on borrowed money decided they'd better sell. Today, so many people were selling, there was hardly anyone to buy—not even the bargain hunters—and a panic set in. Of course, the more stocks are sold, the lower the prices go."

"Is it going to crash?" Rudy said.

"I'm impressed, Rudy," Miss Tibbs said.

"I hope it don't crash!" Little Al said. "Somebody could get hurt!"

Dad chuckled. "I wish it were that kind of crash. We could do something to prevent that. As it is, some bankers have gotten together and contributed a lot of money to try to steady the prices of the leading securities, but a lot of small investors have already lost everything they had." He frowned. "And, of course, the government is calling it mere hysteria and refuses to act in any way."

But Friday and Monday, as Rudy and Hildy Helen made the deliveries for the bakery, people were looking a little more cheerful. The twins heard bits of conversations that sounded hopeful.

"Even if there *were* a recession, the Federal Reserve System would come in and fix it. We'll be all right."

"It's only a temporary slump—not a real depression."

"That's right! It's like a runner catching his breath!"

"Besides, this country's too rich and our business is too big to be bothered much by the stock market anyway."

Rudy didn't understand all of it, but it sounded more promising. Besides, there were other problems on his mind.

On Friday, Rudy took out his shelf in woodworking class to give it the final coat of varnish before he turned it in, only to find three small holes drilled into it. Rudy looked around right away for Maury. He was standing in a far corner, holding a drill and smirking.

On Monday, Mr. Keating asked Rudy to stay after class. When everyone was gone, he said, "Mr. Hutchinson, from what source did you copy your book report?"

"Copy?" Rudy said.

"Don't you realize that copying someone else's work and claiming it as your own is against the law? It's called plagiarism."

"But I didn't copy it," Rudy said. His hands were so wet he could have wrung them out. "That was my work!"

"And I suppose you didn't trace the drawings from that same source."

"No, sir!"

Mr. Keating leaned back against the bookcase under the window and stroked his mustache. "I don't know what to do about this, Mr. Hutchinson."

I know what to do! Rudy wanted to scream. *Believe me!*

"At this point it is nothing more than your word against mine. I just find it hard to believe after all of your clowning around and your eagerness to make light of everything we've done, that you would suddenly come up with a very fine and serious work—especially on a project which is worth such a large portion of your grade. I assume your father is strict about your marks."

Rudy couldn't answer. He was afraid whatever he said would only get him in more trouble.

"Very well, then," Mr. Keating said. "I'm going to have to give this more thought. We'll let it stand as it is for now."

Hildy Helen was waiting for him out in the hall. "What happened?" she said. "Are you in trouble?"

"Not yet," Rudy said. But he felt as if he were. Mr. Keating's doubt was worse than that trip to the principal's office Van had told him to avoid.

What about these *things, Jesus?* Rudy asked that night as he was drawing. *Maury and Mr. Keating? I'm praying. I'm waiting.*

And then he said *Amen*, because there was nothing else he could do.

One thing almost made up for both of those. It happened on Monday, when he and Hildy Helen were riding their bikes back from delivering the last of the day's pies. Hildy Helen suddenly stopped her bike in the middle of the sidewalk. Rudy stopped his, too.

"What?" he said.

"Rudy, why did we ever let ourselves get so far apart from each other?"

Rudy shrugged, but Hildy Helen was insistent.

"I mean it. Why did we?"

"I guess part of it was because you were in your room crying all the time," Rudy said.

"Yeah, and you were always playing pranks or thinking up pranks or—" She shook out her hair. "But it doesn't matter now. What matters is that we have to stay close to each other."

Rudy had to nod.

"I mean it. We aren't just brother and sister—we're *twins*. I almost forgot that till that night at the Ferris wheel when you knew it was the Mob that took Dad on there and nobody else would believe you. But I *knew*, because I know the looks on your face."

LaDonna was wrong about Hildy, Rudy thought. *She doesn't have to dance things out. She has to talk ... and talk ... and talk ...*

"Do you still pray a lot, Rudy?" she said.

"Yeah," Rudy said.

"I've been praying a lot, too. I just go in my room with the door shut and I talk to God ... and talk—"

Rudy had to grin.

"What's so funny?" she said.

"Nothing!" Rudy said.

"Well, you know what I just thought of?"

"No," Rudy said. "But I bet you're about to tell me."

"I just thought of this: You and I pray to the same God."

Rudy considered that. He liked the idea.

"And you know what? When I do get a boyfriend someday—when it's time, like you said—I hope he understands me the way you do, Rudy."

I hope he can listen to you talk as long as I can, Rudy thought as she pedaled off.

And then he followed her, his hands dry on his handlebars.

But the next day the fear crept back in.

It was Tuesday, October 29.

When Hildy Helen and Rudy arrived at the bakery, Ingrid only had a few orders for them to deliver.

"Be extra nice to those people," Oscar said, pointing to the list. "Not many people have a reason to be happy today."

"Now what's happened?" Hildy Helen said as they rode off down Randolph Street.

It didn't take them long to find out. There were newsboys in every block, holding up their papers and yelling, "Read 'em and weep! Bank and Trust Stock Prices Crumble in Record Trading! Crowds at Tickers See Fortunes Wane!"

"What does all that mean, Rudy?" Hildy Helen said.

"I think it means there's been a crash," Rudy said.

The mood in the city was even more disturbing than it had been on Thursday.

When Rudy told the man at the art supply store that the cookies would be 25 cents, the man began to laugh uncontrollably.

"Twenty-five cents?" the man cried. "Sure—I can give you 25 cents! My entire life savings was wiped out today, so what's another 25 cents?"

When they took a birthday cake to a posh apartment on Lake Shore Drive, the little girl in the birthday dress had to give Rudy the money. Her mother was sobbing in the hallway, saying to her husband, "I thought the bankers were going to make it all right!"

"They did what they did for the big trades, dear," he said. "It made no difference to the little investors, and besides—" Rudy heard his voice quaver—"even us big traders went down the drain today."

"But why?"

"Because nobody could buy what so many people were trying to sell. The market has crashed, my dear. We've lost everything."

"That girl isn't going to have a very fun party," Hildy Helen said when they left.

It didn't look as if anyone was going to have a fun party ever again. Rudy was glad when the deliveries had all been made. He wanted to go home and sit in Aunt Gussie's room with a cup of cocoa and listen to Picasso mutter and hear Quintonia complain and even smell Miss Tibbs's cooking. He wanted to be where people hadn't lost all their money, where people trusted him and he could trust them, and where it didn't matter how grown-up he was or wasn't as long as he was trying.

He was starting to pick up speed as they headed back toward the bakery when a long, sleek, Highland green Cadillac pulled up beside him. A woman was driving, and she appeared to be waving at Rudy with a gloved hand.

Rudy didn't recognize her, and he was trying to decide whether to stop for her or not, when behind him Hildy Helen said, "Rudy! That's Dorothea in the backseat! Don't stop!"

A second look at the car revealed not only Dorothea in the back, but Maury in the front. He didn't appear to have seen Rudy yet, because he was scanning the other side of the street with his eyes—eyes that looked different to Rudy than they ever had before. They looked frightened.

The woman in the driver's seat put down her window and leaned out. She was pale, like Dorothea, and her face was thin and almost twisted with fear.

"You're the Hutchinson boy?" she said.

Rudy nodded reluctantly.

"You know my husband, then," she said. "Have you seen him?"

"Today?" Rudy said.

"Yes, this afternoon. Anywhere around here. Have you seen him?"

Rudy could only shake his head. Her voice was scaring him. She sounded as if she were going to begin to scream hysterically any minute.

"If you see him, would you tell us right away?" Mrs. Worthington said.

"Well, sure, I guess so," Rudy said.

"Thank you," she said, and the Cadillac began to move away.

"You're wasting your time, Ma," Rudy heard Maury say. "He ain't never gonna help us!"

"They hate us!" Dorothea said from the backseat.

"What was *that* all about?" Hildy Helen said when they had driven away.

"I don't know," Rudy said.

He was shaking again as they rode on, but it didn't feel so much like fear this time. There had just been something not quite right about Mrs. Worthington and Maury and Dorothea. They had looked as if they had just had something sucked out of them and they were searching for whatever that was as much as they were looking for Mr. Worthington. Rudy felt empty, in that shaky way he sometimes felt when he was hungry.

They had nearly reached the Wabash Street bridge by then. It was growing gray and chilly, and Rudy wanted to get back home more than ever. But Hildy Helen stopped her bike at the bottom of the bridge and pointed toward the top.

"Rudy," she said, "what is that man doing?"

"I don't know," Rudy said without looking. "I just want to go—"

"No, Rudy! He's climbing up onto the railing!"

Rudy jerked his head around in time to see a tall, bulky figure in an overcoat swinging his second leg over the bridge railing. He sat on it, swinging his feet down over the river, like an overgrown boy about to jump into a swimming hole.

"You don't think he's going to jump, do you?" Hildy Helen said. "Would he get hurt?"

"I don't *know*!" Rudy said. He knew he'd snapped out the words in an angry way, but this was reminding him too much of Dad being held over the railing, being dropped over the side—

"Maybe we ought to get somebody, like a policeman," Hildy Helen said.

"Yeah, let's go do that," Rudy said.

Hildy Helen turned her bicycle around. Rudy was about to follow, when he took one last look at the man. The hulking figure was just removing his hat. Rudy watched in horror as he held it out over the river and dropped it in. The man's face was in full view now.

It was Maury Worthington's father.

Chapter Seventeen

*A*re you coming?" Hildy Helen called to him.

Rudy could only shake his head. The rest of him was frozen for the moment.

Maury Worthington's father—that big, threatening bully of a man—was getting ready to jump from a bridge?

Rudy took a step backward with his bike. *If I go up and say anything to him, he's liable to pull me in with him!* he thought. *Hildy Helen's right. We should just go get somebody.*

But then Mr. Worthington leaned forward, and Rudy saw the image of his own father being pushed forward over that same river from a bridge just as high.

This was somebody else's father. No matter how rotten that somebody else could be, Rudy knew how Maury and Dorothea would feel if that man jumped. He knew because he had felt it himself.

Rudy got off his bike and let it fall against the railing at the end of the bridge.

"Where are you going?" Hildy Helen said.

Rudy didn't answer but walked as quickly as he could toward Mr. Worthington without breaking into a run. He waited until he was close enough to him to get a hand on his sleeve before he said, "Sir? Please don't jump."

Mr. Worthington whipped his head toward Rudy and looked right at him. But Rudy was sure Mr. Worthington didn't see him— or anything else. His eyes were glazed, just the way Aunt Gussie's had been when she had her stroke.

"Why shouldn't I?" Mr. Worthington said to the person he wasn't seeing. "Why shouldn't I jump? I've lost everything. My family will hate me. No, I want to die."

With Rudy's hand still gripping his arm, he leaned forward again.

"Rudy?" Hildy Helen said from somewhere very close.

"Grab him!" Rudy said.

Hildy Helen did, throwing herself around Mr. Worthington's other arm. Rudy did the same on the other side, and they both swayed out over the river as the big man leaned forward.

"No, don't!" Rudy cried. "Pull him back, Hildy!"

Hildy put her full weight behind the shove away from the railing, and so did Rudy. Mr. Worthington was caught off balance, and he tumbled clumsily from the railing to the bridge with Rudy and Hildy Helen on top of him. A car swerved to miss them, blaring its horn, and kept going.

"Come on, sir," Rudy said. "Get up. We're gonna get you home. We'll take him to the bakery," he said to Hildy Helen. "And we'll call his house from there."

Hildy Helen nodded as Mr. Worthington allowed them to bring him to his feet. He looked down at her, and tears formed in his eyes. "I've lost everything, Dorothea," he said to her.

Hildy Helen's eyes widened, and she looked at Rudy.

"It's okay, Dad," Rudy said.

"It's okay, Maury?" he said.

"Sure. I don't care about the money."

"I don't either, Daddy," Hildy Helen said. "Let's just go home."

The big, confused man cried quietly all the way down Wacker Drive to LaSalle Street. Just as they were about to turn down Randolph, the green Cadillac pulled up to the curb.

"Here's your husband," Rudy said to the thin woman who got out of the front seat and stumbled to him. He knew it was a stupid thing to say, but what was there to say to a woman whose husband didn't even know who anyone was?

Rudy didn't look at Maury as they drove away. He wouldn't have wanted anyone looking at him if it had been his father.

It was true. The stock market had crashed that day, October 29. Rudy listened to it all on the radio and went in to inform Aunt Gussie.

"More than 16 million shares were sold today alone," he told her. "Stocks that were sold for $100 a share last week were dumped for $3 today."

Aunt Gussie moaned sadly.

"I thought you'd be saying, 'I told you so!'" Rudy said.

Aunt Gussie shook her head and picked up her pencil. "Whole fortunes have been wiped out," she wrote. "I'm sorry for people."

Rudy thought of Mr. Worthington. "Me, too," he said.

Then Aunt Gussie wrote, "It's going to affect us all."

"It is?" Rudy said.

"Ya, Ru," she said.

Rudy nodded his head and grinned. Maybe it would, but right now, nothing mattered as much as Aunt Gussie almost talking again.

"I like that name, Ru," he said. "I think I'll keep it."

Aunt Gussie was right, of course. The stock market crash did affect all of them—and in ways Rudy couldn't ever have predicted.

The next day in the gymnasium, Rudy saw Maury coming toward him before the lineup, and he tried not to cringe, at least on the outside. This was a threat coming if he ever saw one: *You tell anybody what my father almost did and you'll get it, Hutchinson.*

But when Maury got to him, he could barely look Rudy in the eye.

"Hey, Hutchinson," he said.

"Maury, I'm not gonna tell anybody about your father, all right? I promise."

Maury looked up with his lower lip hanging. "Huh?" he said.

"About your dad—"

"Yeah, about my dad," Maury said. "Thanks. Y'know, for savin' his life."

He had made the entire speech to the floor, and Rudy, too, pointed his face downward and said, "It's all right. Maybe you'da done the same for me."

Maury grunted. And then he walked away, still looking at the floorboards, as if he weren't sure about that at all, and he didn't like realizing it.

Well, whatta ya know, Rudy thought.

His next surprise came right after lunch, when everyone was hurrying to clubs for activities period. Little Al was waiting outside the Argosy Club room, shuffling his feet around. The way he was looking at the floor, Rudy wondered if this was the beginning of a new trend.

"Aren't you going to orchestra practice?" Rudy said.

"Yeah," Little Al said. "But I wanted to give you this first, Rudolpho."

He held out a paper sack to Rudy.

"What's this?" Rudy said.

"Look inside."

Rudy took it carefully, and Little Al gave a nervous laugh. "Don't worry. It's not gonna bite ya."

Rudy grinned at him and plunged his hand into the bag. He pulled it out full of money—dollar bills and change. And there was more in the bottom of the bag. There must have been 10 dollars there.

"Where'd you get all this?" Rudy said.

"Shinin' shoes," Little Al said. "Them businessmen on the Northside, they're big tippers, 'specially if you listen to all their problems—give 'em the old sympathetic ear, if you know what I mean."

"What are you gonna do with it?"

"I'm givin' it to you," Little Al said. "So's you can get yer pictures printed in that magazine, be a real member of the club, all that stuff."

Rudy felt his chin dropping as he shook his head. "I can't take all your money. You earned this!"

"And I guess I can do anything I want with it. And what I wanna do is give it to you." Little Al's gaze went back to the floor. "Yer the best person I know, Rudolpho. Yer the whole reason I went to work in the first place."

"But I'd feel so guilty, I—"

"Aw, dummy up, would ya, Rudolpho? And go give the money to that fella before I gotta do it for ya."

Then they grinned at each other. That afternoon, Rudy became an official member of the Argosy Club, with money left over. That, they decided, would be saved for an outing for all three of the kids.

But the results of the crash didn't stop there. In fact, they had only begun.

About two weeks later, Dad gathered the whole family in Aunt Gussie's room for a meeting. They were all there, including Picasso, who muttered happily from his cage and let out the occasional, "Gustavia Nitz!" in joyful tones.

"So what's up, Mr. Hutchie?" Little Al said.

Dad wasted no time.

"I want to reassure all of you that Aunt Gussie and I have lost nothing in the stock market crash. Neither one of us ever invested, and Aunt Gussie took her money out of the banks some months ago. However, the collapse is going to affect everyone. It already has. Most people hadn't taken their money out of the banks, and the banks were investing their funds in the stock market. When the market crashed, the banks had nothing to give their customers. So not only have the investors lost their money, but the middle class and the poor have been wiped out as well. It's a real financial disaster, my dears."

"So, what does all of that mean, Mr. Jim?" LaDonna said.

"It means the party of the 1920s is over. President Hoover keeps trying to tell us that the stock market is going to swing up again, but I just don't think that's going to happen. Thirty billion dollars has blown away into thin air. Many people can't pay their bills. Workers are already losing jobs because companies don't need them—because not many people can afford to buy the goods they make or the services they provide."

"Is this what they mean by a depression?" Rudy said. "I heard people talking about it that day."

"It's a depression, all right," Dad said. "In more ways than one. If people don't have faith in God, it's going to be overwhelming."

"Are we going to be poor?" Hildy Helen said.

"Aunt Gussie has always been wise with her money. We'll be provided for, but we aren't going to have some of the luxuries we've been enjoying since we came here."

"We have five dollars we've saved," Rudy said. "And you can have all the money I make."

"Count me in, Mr. Hutchie," Little Al said. "I kinda like shinin' shoes."

"I could find a job, too," Hildy Helen said.

"And I don't have to go to college right away," LaDonna said.

Dad was looking at them all with his eyes shining behind his glasses. "I'm proud of you kids," he said. "And we're going to see to it that none of you has to give up your dreams. Right, Auntie?"

Aunt Gussie nodded and gave one of her rare smiles—well, half a smile. "Ri—" she said. And then she pointed to each of the children, one at a time. Rudy was sure he had never felt so loved.

"And how about you, Effa?" Dad said. "Are you and I in agreement about all this?"

Hildy Helen looked at Rudy, and he could read the question in her eyes: *Why does Miss Tibbs have to be in agreement?*

LaDonna seemed to be having the same eye-conversation with Quintonia. "Are you trying to tell us something, Mr. Jim?" she said.

"Yes, I am," Dad said. He reached for Miss Tibbs, and she snuggled in under his arm. "Miss Tibbs and I are going to be married."

Aunt Gussie was the first to recover from the surprised silence that followed. "Goo—" she said. She was bobbing her head and holding out her hand to Miss Tibbs.

"Well, hot dog!" Little Al said. "I always said I liked a doll like you, Miss Tibbsy. You're welcome to the family, is what I say."

"Me, too," Hildy Helen said. She beamed around the room. "This family just keeps getting bigger and bigger!"

Rudy was glad no one asked him what he thought. He tried to smile his way through the rest of the meeting, and then went up to his room to draw. It wasn't that he didn't like Miss Tibbs. He'd begun to resent her less and less since Aunt Gussie started to get better. But to have her as part of the *family*? She was always pushing him to be better and do better. That kind of pressure only added to his fears that he would mess everything up.

Or maybe it wasn't that. Maybe it was just too much change, just when he'd been about to figure things out.

He didn't figure it out that night. He didn't even figure it out for a long time after that. But at least the next day, he got one *piece* that made him feel more at ease until he *could* make sense of it.

In English class, Mr. Keating announced that he was handing back the book reports. Rudy's heart pounded in his ears. It had been two weeks since Mr. Keating had accused him of cheating, and since then he hadn't said a word about it. What mark was he going to see on his paper? What if he failed?

What if he had to go through the rest of the year with Mr. Keating thinking he was a cheater?

That feeling built up again—the one where he felt as if he were going to burst open. He let his eyes close, and he pictured Jesus telling him that it would be all right—even if he had to wait for it.

"Mr. Hutchinson?"

Mr. Keating was standing next to his desk, holding Rudy's book report in his hand. Rudy looked down at his desk. He was afraid to try to read Mr. Keating's eyes.

"I owe you an apology for waiting so long to tell you my decision," Mr. Keating said.

Please don't wait any longer, Rudy thought.

"And I also apologize for doubting your word."

He put the book report on Rudy's desk. A large red A stared back up at him.

"I have been reviewing all the work you have turned in since this paper," Mr. Keating went on, "and I have found all of it to be of the same high quality as this project. Besides—"

He cleared his throat in such a nervous way that Rudy had to look up at him. Now *he* was carefully watching the floor.

"I spoke with Miss Tibbs just yesterday. I ran into her at a city-wide teachers' meeting, and I mentioned my concern over your book report." Mr. Keating's mustache twitched. "She informed me in no uncertain terms that she herself had seen you working on both the report and the drawings night after night in your home."

There was a pause, and Rudy was sure he was supposed to say something, but he couldn't imagine what. Besides, he was thinking something very far from his book report. He was thinking, *Maybe it won't be so bad having Miss Tibbs for a stepmother after all.* As the day went on, the maybe got smaller. By the time he got to work, he'd made a decision.

He hurried through his deliveries. As Oscar had predicted, business was getting lighter, and there weren't very many of them. Rudy watched the Feilchenfelds when he returned to the bakery, but neither Oscar nor Sylvia seemed disturbed. Oscar kept baking. Sylvia kept frosting cakes and smiling. Rudy went to her and said, "Would you help me decorate a cake? I won't take any pay this week if you will."

"What kind of cake?" she said, still smiling, of course.

"Uh, an engagement cake."

"You're a good boy!" Sylvia said. "A nice big diamond ring? Or maybe some flowers? Some of your roses?"

"No, I think I want to paint a prayer on it."

Sylvia's smile grew puzzled. "A prayer?" she said.

"Like this." Rudy picked up a pencil and quickly sketched the idea that had been brewing while he made his deliveries. It was simple. It was Jesus' hands, folded, calmly waiting. He thought Dad and Miss Tibbs would understand.

He wasn't sure Sylvia did. She was smiling in a befuddled kind of way when she went off to the kitchen for more food coloring. Ingrid took that opportunity to look over Rudy's shoulder at the sketch.

"This is just my opinion, Hutchinson," she said.

"Do I have to hear it?" Rudy said.

"Well, I was just going to say that Miss Tibbs is lucky to be marrying a Hutchinson man."

"Oh," Rudy said.

"Matter of fact, if you were a little older, Rudy, I'd marry you."

Rudy's face immediately began to burn, and he didn't know where to put his eyes. Behind him, Ingrid chuckled.

"I didn't mean to embarrass you, Hutchinson," she said.

"I'm not embarrassed!" Rudy said.

"Yes, you are!"

"No, I'm not. I'll prove it!"

Rudy scooped up a fingerful of frosting and let it fly, square onto Ingrid's freckled nose. It only stopped her for a second before she was laughing and gathering up a handful of cake icing and smearing it playfully all over Rudy's face.

"Oh, yeah?" he said. "How about this?" And he plastered a glob on her earlobe.

She was in the process of painting his hair with the remains when Sylvia let out a bellow from the doorway.

"What?" she said. "In the window?"

"Sorry, Mama!" Ingrid said.

She picked up the frosting bowl and ran toward the kitchen. Rudy was hot on her trail.

"We're not finished yet!" Rudy cried.

"Says you!" Ingrid said.

And they burst past a bewildered Sylvia, frosting dripping and mouths grinning.

I'm being a kid! Rudy thought happily. *Things are gettin' harder and there's a lot of waiting around for stuff, but I can still be a kid.*

He thought of the folded hands he was going to paint on the cake for Dad and Miss Tibbs. They were Jesus-hands, he decided. And they were the same hands that were going to help him learn to grow up in the hard times ahead. After all, Dad was still in trouble with the Mob. And Rudy himself had a long way to go before he would be grown up. There would be lots more worrying about all the responsibility and people depending on him. But with God's help, he'd try to live up to it all.

But I can still be a kid, he thought. And one thing he knew for sure: He would always—always—be God's kid.

✠ ⬥ ✠

There's More Adventure in the CHRISTIAN HERITAGE SERIES!

The Salem Years, 1689–1691

The Rescue #1

Josiah Hutchinson's sister Hope is terribly ill. Can a stranger—whose presence could destroy the family's relationship with everyone else in Salem Village—save her?

The Stowaway #2

Josiah's dream of becoming a sailor seems within reach. But will the evil schemes of a tough orphan named Simon land Josiah and his sister in a heap of trouble?

The Guardian #3

Josiah has a plan to deal with the wolves threatening the town. Can he carry it out without endangering himself—or Cousin Rebecca, who'll follow him anywhere?

The Accused #4

Robbed by the cruel Putnam brothers, Josiah suddenly finds himself on trial for crimes he didn't commit. Can he convince anyone of his innocence?

The Samaritan #5

Josiah tries to help a starving widow and her daughter. But will his feud with the Putnams wreck everything he's worked for?

The Secret #6

If Papa finds out who Hope's been sneaking away to see, he'll be furious! Josiah knows her secret; should he tell?

The Williamsburg Years, 1780–1781

The Rebel #1

Josiah's great-grandson, Thomas Hutchinson, didn't rob the apothecary shop where he works. So why does he wind up in jail, and will he ever get out?

The Thief #2

Someone's stealing horses in Williamsburg! But is the masked rider Josiah sees the real culprit, and who's behind the mask?

The Burden #3

Thomas knows secrets he can't share. So what can he do when a crazed Walter Clark holds him at gunpoint over a secret he doesn't even know?

The Prisoner #4

As war rages in Williamsburg, Thomas' mentor refuses to fight and is carried off by the Patriots. Now which side will Thomas choose?

The Invasion #5

Word comes that Benedict Arnold and his men are ransacking plantations. Can Thomas and his family protect their homestead—even when it's invaded by British soldiers who take Caroline as a hostage?

The Battle #6

Thomas is surrounded by war! Can he tackle still another fight, taking orders from a woman he doesn't like—and being forbidden to talk about his missing brother?

The Charleston Years, 1860–1861

The Misfit #1

When the crusade to abolish slavery reaches full swing, Thomas Hutchinson's great-grandson Austin is sent to live with slave-holding relatives. How can he ever fit in?

The Ally #2

Austin resolves to teach young slave Henry-James to read, even though it's illegal. If Uncle Drayton finds out, will both boys pay the ultimate price?

The Threat #3

Trouble follows Austin to Uncle Drayton's vacation home. Who are those two men Austin hears scheming against his uncle—and why is a young man tampering with the family stagecoach?

The Trap #4

Austin's slave friend Henry-James beats hired hand Narvel in a wrestling match. Will Narvel get the revenge he seeks by picking fights and trapping Austin in a water well?

The Hostage #5

As north and south move toward civil war, Austin is kidnapped by men determined to stop his father from preaching against slavery. Can he escape?

The Escape #6

With the Civil War breaking out, Austin tries to keep Uncle Drayton from selling Henry-James at the slave auction. Will it work, and can Austin flee South Carolina with the rest of the Hutchinsons before Confederate soldiers find them?

The Chicago Years, 1928–1929

The Trick #1

Rudy and Hildy Helen Hutchinson and their father move to Chicago to live with their rich great-aunt Gussie. Can they survive the bullies they find—not to mention Little Al, a young schemer with hopes of becoming a mobster?

The Chase #2

Rudy and his family face one problem after another—including an accident that sends Rudy to the doctor, and the disappearance of Little Al. But can they make it through a deadly dispute between the mob and the Ku Klux Klan?

The Capture #3

It's Christmastime, but Rudy finds nothing to celebrate. Will his attorney father's defense of a Jewish boy accused of murder—and Hildy Helen's kidnapping—ruin far more than the holiday?

The Stunt #4

Rudy gets in trouble wing-walking on a plane. But can he stay standing as he finds himself in the middle of a battle for racial equality—and Aunt Gussie's dangerous fight for workers' rights?

The Caper #5

Strange things are going on at Cape Cod, where Rudy and his family are vacationing. What's in a mysterious trunk found on the beach, and who are those shadowy men in a boat who seem to be carrying . . . bodies?

The Pursuit #6

A deadly warning from the mob . . . Aunt Gussie felled by a stroke . . . impending stock market disaster! Rudy just wants to be a kid, but events won't let him. Will his faith be enough to get him through it all?

Available at a Christian bookstore near you

FOCUS ON THE FAMILY®

Like this book?

Then you'll love *Clubhouse* magazine! It's written for kids just like you, and it's loaded with great stories, interesting articles, puzzles, games, and fun things for you to do. Some issues include posters, too! With your parents' permission, we'll even send you a complimentary copy.

Simply write to Focus on the Family, Colorado Springs, CO 80995 (in Canada, write P.O. 9800, Stn. Terminal, Vancouver, B.C. V6B 4G3) and mention that you saw this offer in the back of this book. Or, call 1-800-A-FAMILY (in Canada, call 1-800-661-9800).

You may also visit our Web site (www.family.org) to learn more about the ministry or find out if there is a Focus on the Family office in your country.

• • •

"Adventures in Odyssey" is a fantastic series of books, videos, and radio dramas that's fun for the entire family—parents, too! You'll love the twists and turns found in the novels, as well as the excitement packed into every video. And the 30 albums of radio dramas (available on audiocassette or compact disc) are great to listen to in the car, after dinner . . . even at bedtime! You can hear "Adventures in Odyssey" on the radio, too. Call Focus on the Family for a listing of local stations airing these programs or to request any of the "Adventures in Odyssey" resources. They're also available at Christian bookstores everywhere.

Focus on the Family is an organization that is dedicated to helping you and your family establish lasting, loving relationships with each other and the Lord. It's why we exist! If we can assist you or your family in any way, please feel free to contact us. We'd love to hear from you!